Holy hell, he couldn't seem to control himself around her...

"Lose the T-shirt." Wren flicked her hand in Rhys's direction. "It needs to come off."

He hesitated for a moment, but the lust in her eyes urged him on. He peeled the soaked cotton up and over his head.

"The jeans, too," Wren said, keeping her face straight. "They're soaked."

Rhys glanced down and saw a small dark patch where the denim had absorbed the water. They were hardly soaked. "You sure about that?"

"Let me help you." She stepped forward and reached for the buckle on his belt.

Her fingertips grazed the bare skin of his stomach and he had to stifle a moan.

He might have started the fire, but she was fanning the flames...

Dear Reader,

I'm thrilled to be continuing The Dangerous Bachelors Club series with Harlequin Blaze. This means there will be plenty more steamy stories with a dash of suspense coming your way.

If you've been following this series, you may remember Rhys from *A Dangerously Sexy Affair*. In that book he plays a slightly antagonistic role and I wasn't initially planning to give him a book. But that's how it is with some characters—they get under your skin and beg to have their story told.

Who am I to say no to a character in need of a happy ending?

Rhys has a strong sense of what he believes in. Everything he does fits in with his personal motto, "tough but fair." He lives via this rigid code, and everything he does is to the highest standard possible. Then the heroine comes along and makes his life messy in the best ways possible.

The relationship between Rhys and Wren is very much about finding balance and common ground. I love the idea of two people who seem so completely opposite coming together to see that they're actually perfectly suited to one another. They're like pieces of a jigsaw puzzle.

I really hope you enjoy Wren and Rhys's story. You can find out what's coming next by checking out my website, stefanie-london.com, or on Facebook at Facebook.com/StefanieLondonAuthor. I love chatting with readers, so feel free to drop me a line anytime.

With love,

Stefanie

Stefanie London

A Dangerously Sexy Secret

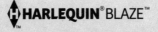

Recycling programs
for this product may
not exist in your area.

ISBN-13: 978-0-373-79918-3

A Dangerously Sexy Secret

Copyright © 2016 by Stefanie Little

Printed in U.S.A.

USA TODAY bestselling author **Stefanie London** is a voracious reader who has dreamed of being an author her whole life. After sneaking several English-lit subjects into her "very practical" business degree, she got a job in corporate communications. But it wasn't long before she turned to romance fiction. She recently left her hometown of Melbourne to start a new adventure in Toronto and now spends her days writing contemporary romances with humor, heat and heart.

For more information on Stefanie and her books, check out her website at stefanie-london.com or her Facebook page at Facebook.com/stefanielondonauthor.

Books by Stefanie London

Harlequin Blaze

The Dangerous Bachelors Club

A Dangerously Sexy Christmas
A Dangerously Sexy Affair

Harlequin Kiss

Breaking the Bro Code
Only the Brave Try Ballet

Harlequin Presents

The Tycoon's Stowaway

To get the inside scoop on Harlequin Blaze and its talented writers, visit Facebook.com/BlazeAuthors.

All backlist available in ebook format.

Visit the Author Profile page at Harlequin.com for more titles.

To Dad,
for all the important lessons you taught me.
For pushing me to be a good student.
For fostering my creativity.
And for sitting through all my ballet concerts. I
know they were really long.

1

WREN LIVINGSTON COULD MULTITASK, there was no doubt about it. But carrying four bags of groceries while walking up a flight of stairs in a maxi skirt *and* trying to deflect sisterly guilt was pushing it. Even for her.

Add to the mix the fact that her new and insanely hot next-door neighbor was coming down the hallway toward her, and Wren was at her limit. How was one supposed to carry on a normal conversation with all those muscles staring back at you? Impossible.

"Sis?" Debbie whined on the other end of the phone. "Are you even listening to me?"

"Uh-huh." Wren watched as the guy stopped in front of her, his pearly smile gleaming bright against warm brown skin. The black tail of his headphones curved up from an armband sitting snugly over his biceps.

Oh yeah, muscles... Had she mentioned them? He had a lot.

"Can I give you a hand with those bags?" he asked, pulling one bud from his ear.

He must have been about to go for a run, if the gray shorts and navy cotton tank were anything to go on. The fabric hugged a solid chest and caught her eye, drawing her attention up until she set her sights on a sharp jaw, broad nose and sparkling warm brown eyes.

Sweet mother of…

"Oh." She shook her head, cheeks fiery hot as she realized she must have been gaping at him. "No, I'm fine. Very fine. I mean…uhh…thank you."

"You sure?"

"Absolutely sure. One hundred percent." A nervous giggle bubbled up in her throat that she tried to tamp down—and failed. The fizzy sound burst out and she cringed.

Total brain cell destruction in three, two, one…

"Okay, then." His voice was rich and deep, smooth like satin sheets.

He stuck the bud back into his ear and gave her space to shuffle awkwardly past him in the tight hallway. Her shopping bags knocked against the wall and she almost tripped on the sweeping hem of her skirt.

Can you at least stay upright for the next three minutes so you don't embarrass yourself? You're walking like a drunk llama.

She told herself not to turn around and look back at him. But she couldn't resist. Her mouth dried up when her gaze landed on the wide expanse of his shoulders as he jogged down the stairs.

"What was *that* all about?" Debbie asked, and Wren realized her sister was still on the phone. "Since when do you giggle like a little girl?"

"It's nothing." She wedged the phone between her ear and shoulder as she reached the front door of her new apartment. "Nothing at all."

Let's keep it at nothing—you're not here to ogle men.

Her arm ached from carrying all the shopping bags in one hand, the burn in her muscles getting hotter as she fumbled for her keys. Sweat beaded at her hairline. What in the world had possessed her to move into a building with no elevator?

"Didn't sound like nothing."

"Debbie…" Wren sighed as she pushed the door open with a grunt. "It was just my neighbor."

"What's he like?"

Delicious. The word sprang to her mind immediately. The guy from apartment 401 was definitely all that and a bag of chips, as her old boss used to say. So far she hadn't done more than return his friendly hellos and now turn down his offer of help in a most embarrassing way. But she'd be lying if she said he hadn't made an appearance in one—okay, two…at least—dirty dreams.

"He seems nice. Friendly." She let out a silent gasp of relief as she set the bags on the kitchen counter. "Same as everyone else here."

"And where is *here*, exactly?" Debbie's tone was sharp. "You still haven't told me where you're staying."

"I'm in New York."

"New York is a big place. How about you narrow it down to a borough for me?"

Her sister was exactly the kind of person who would show up on her doorstep, wanting to "help" and be part of the action. But Debbie, while she was a great person and the shining star of the Livingston family, was not exactly street smart. Or subtle.

"I don't want anyone else getting involved." She turned and sagged back against the counter, pushing her hair from her eyes.

"*You* shouldn't be involved," her sister huffed.

Maybe. But her best friend, Kylie, had been attacked and she refused to talk about it.

Wren had a strong suspicion the incident had something to do with the gallery where Kylie had been working because anytime Wren mentioned it, Kylie went white as a ghost.

Originally they had both applied for the gallery internship, but only Kylie had been successful in gaining one of the coveted spots. Then, after she returned home, the gallery's owner had called Wren to offer her Kylie's old spot. Seems she'd been next in line.

And just like that, Wren had packed her bags and moved to New York.

"I still can't believe you've gone on this vigilante mission," Debbie continued. "Now *I* have to miss out on seeing my sister because you've once again taken on other people's problems. I can't even send you a goddamn Christmas card."

"It's not even June yet. Christmas is ages away and things will be back to normal by then… I promise." She spoke the words with way more confidence than she felt. "As for Kylie—"

"I'll look after her, I promise." Debbie sighed. "Although I have no idea how I'm supposed to keep dodging her questions about where you've run off to. She knows something's up."

"We stick to the story—I'm away at an art retreat and they have a no-cell-phone policy, so she can't call. But I'll email her when I can. No one else needs to know what I'm doing, got it?"

Debbie grumbled her agreement. They lived in a small town where information had a way of traveling at the speed of light. The only reason she'd revealed more of her plan to Debbie was because her sister had caught her booking a flight to New York after she'd said the retreat was in California.

"If I get in trouble here I don't want to drag anyone else into my problems."

"Don't you mean *Kylie's* problems?"

"Come on, Deb." She sighed. "Kylie is like our sister. I *have* to find out what happened to her. Anyway, my reputation is already ruined at home… What do I have to lose by trying to do something good for a friend?"

"Your reputation is not ruined. A few uptight old biddies think you're a bit wild, so what?"

"They called me a sexual deviant." Her humiliation still burned as brightly as a newly lit flame. "And a blight on their community."

"It's not true. You've helped out so many families at the community center, you've painted faces at the summer fair," Debbie said, and Wren could practically see her sister ticking the items off her perfectly manicured fingers the way she always did when she was mad. "You've made cupcakes for almost every bake sale and your stuff is *always* the first to sell out, you've—"

"Enough." She drew a deep breath and closed her eyes for a moment. Never in her life would she admit how much it hurt that Charity Springs had ostracized her, and hearing her sister point out all she'd done was only making it worse.

She may not be the biggest fan of the small town—or its residents—but it was still her home.

"Debs, please. Can we not rehash this again? I know you're upset with me for leaving and I'm sorry. But I need to do this."

"You 'need' to run around fixing other people's problems, do you? All right, I guess you do." It was as close to acceptance as Wren was going to get, so she'd take it. "What are you supposed to do, spend your days playing spy?"

"I'm working at a gallery and I'm painting. It's not exactly a hard life." She didn't bother to mention the recon activities she was planning, like trying to break into her new boss's email account.

Details. You're doing the right thing by your friend—that's all that matters.

Debbie made a scoffing sound on the other end of the line. "You're so full of shit."

"And you swear way too much for a girl who's going to be an upstanding pillar of society." Wren began to unpack her groceries. Flour for her pizza base, some fresh kale, tomatoes, basil and a delicious-looking knob of buffalo mozzarella.

"Upstanding pillar of society?" Debbie snorted. "Spare me. And I've noticed that your little list of activities doesn't involve screwing your hot neighbor."

Heat crawled up Wren's cheeks. Thank God she'd decided not to video chat with her sister, because she was sure her face would be flaming tomato red right about now. "I never mentioned he was hot."

"That heavy breathing did all the talking for you." Her sister cackled. "Not to mention the fact that you seemed to forget how to string a sentence together as soon as he came near you."

Usually, she didn't engage in her sister's teasing, but right now she was grateful that the conversation had turned away from her secret mission. "Okay, he's good-looking. So what? That's not reason enough for me to sleep with him."

"Isn't it? When was the last time you got laid? And if you tell me that you haven't had sex since you broke up with Christian, so help me…"

For someone who was supposedly a "sexual deviant," she'd actually been quite conservative when it came to sex. There'd been no one in the six months since she'd broken up with her ex—because now all the men in town either thought she was easy or bad news. Neither of which was true.

Sucking on her lower lip, she concentrated on continuing to unpack the groceries. Milk, eggs, butter, vanilla extract.

"Wren?"

A spring-form pan, parchment paper, confectioners' sugar. "Yeah?"

"Really?"

"You said not to tell you if I hadn't…"

"Are you serious?"

"The only guys interested in me now are the ones I don't want." She slammed the box of granola down on the counter harder than necessary. "And I'm not ready to try opening up to anyone else, not after the way Christian humiliated me."

"You're never going to be ready until you take a risk. You have to put yourself out there. Listen to me, I'm a doctor."

Wren gritted her teeth. "First, you don't get to say you're a doctor until you finish med school. Second, why do you care so much about my sex life?"

"Because you're my sister and you deserve to *have* a sex life. You're twenty-six, for crying out loud, not a hundred and six. But if you don't get some action your vagina will dry up like an old prune."

Despite herself, Wren let out a burst of laughter.

"It's a fact. A *medical* fact. Trust me, I'm a doctor." This time Debbie said the words through her own giggles. "Do you want a pruney va—"

"Shut up." Wren shook her head and bundled up the empty plastic bags. "I'm not having sex with the first guy I see just for the sake of it."

"Seriously, you need to stop hiding away because a few people said bad, *untrue* things. You deserve to live a full life. Orgasms included."

"How do you know my neighbor will be good enough to give me orgasms?" Flashes of her dream from last night came back to her—Mr. 401's large hands roaming her body, his full, wide mouth covering her breasts.

Dammit. It wasn't right to fantasize about a guy without knowing his name.

"Judging by the crazy way you were giggling, I think he will." Debbie sounded smug as hell, the evil little thing. "Trust me, you won't regret it. Sex is a very natural and healthy part of life. It's good for your brain and your heart. You're really doing your health a disservice by *not* having sex."

"Is that another medical fact?" She grinned in spite of herself and shook her head. Her sister knew exactly how to push her buttons and get under her skin, but they always looked out for each other. No matter what.

"Yep, I'm sure it's in one of my textbooks. I have to go. I've got a study session planned and the last person there has to buy coffee." She paused. "I miss you, Birdie."

At the sound of her childhood nickname, Wren smiled. "I miss you, too. I'll be home soon. I promise."

"You'd better."

She hung up the phone and steadied herself against

the countertop. Debbie had a point. Her life had been filled with nothing but stress the last few months; maybe it wouldn't be so bad to live a little.

So long as living doesn't involve any promises or commitment. You're done with that crap!

Totally done. She'd trusted her ex, had even flirted with the idea of getting hitched in the late darkness of night when she'd curled up against him. But it turned out that she hadn't really known him at all…and he clearly hadn't known her.

She wouldn't put herself in a position to be ripped apart like that again. But she could still have some fun… right?

Wren drew a knife from the wooden block next to her stove and placed it on her cutting board. She didn't have to make any decisions right now. She would be in New York for at least a month, so she could take her time. Maybe talk to Mr. 401 a little more before she made a move.

But first she had a pizza to make; she wasn't in the habit of doing any serious thinking on an empty stomach.

RHYS GLOVER ROUNDED the last corner of his run, dodging a couple with linked arms as he pounded his feet into the pavement. He loved nothing more than getting fresh air on the weekend, be it running, biking or otherwise. He put long hours into his job—which he wouldn't trade for anything—but it didn't exactly make for an active or healthy lifestyle during the week.

So Saturdays and Sundays were all about getting out of the house. Getting his blood pumping and his heart racing. Getting his sweat on.

You might be able to do a few of those things indoors if you had the stones to ask Blondie on a date.

He shook his head as he slowed to a stop in front of his walk-up, detouring to collect his mail. Blondie—aka the smoking-hot fox who'd recently moved into the apartment across from him—occupied far too much of his headspace lately. But, try as he might to evict her image from his mind, the waist-length hair that shimmered like spun gold and those long limbs tempted him beyond belief. Rhys prided himself on being a man of solid self-control, but one glance at her and he was as horny as a teenager.

Chiding himself, he shoved the key into his box. A small stack of letters sat inside, mostly bills. A bright blue envelope caught his attention. It bore his stepbrother's neat, utilitarian print and the childish scrawl of his niece. A happy face decorated one corner. They insisted on sending him a real birthday card, even when he told them he was happy with an email or phone call. A wave of jealousy ghosted through him.

It wasn't fair to resent his stepbrother, Marc, for the perfect, happy life he'd been gifted. But it was hard not to compare. Or compete. They were the same age and had grown up together as best friends before their parents had gotten hitched. He'd always envied how easily everything came to Marc—grades, girls, sports. *Everything.*

And now, as adults, Marc still had the edge. He'd given their parents two grandchildren and he had a beautiful wife whom he adored. Marc often joked that he envied Rhys his bachelor lifestyle, but Rhys didn't believe it for a second.

Rhys knew part of the reason he felt compelled to settle down was because it was the one thing Marc had over him. In their parents' eyes, he'd achieved the dream. Happy wife, two healthy kids…and Rhys was still lagging behind, as always.

But it was hard to have a relationship when he didn't even put himself out there. He was just too busy with work to meet people.

"You don't even know if Blondie's single," he muttered to himself as he started up the stairs.

But she hadn't looked at him the way a woman in a committed relationship would when they'd almost bumped into one another earlier.

The pink blush that had crept into her cheeks had done crazy things to him. The kind of crazy things that were not so easily concealed in a pair of running shorts.

The fourth floor was deserted, and Rhys couldn't stop himself from glancing at number 402 as he walked up to the door of his own apartment. Maybe he should formally introduce himself? It would be the neighborly thing to do.

He glanced down at his sweat-soaked tank and shorts. It might be the neighborly thing to do, but he wasn't exactly going to make a great impression if he knocked on her door smelling like a locker room.

Tomorrow.

Satisfied that he'd committed himself to an action, he pushed open the door to his apartment with his free hand. Toeing off his sneakers, he hung his keys on their designated hook and placed the letters into the inbox he kept on the bureau near his desk. All except the blue envelope, which he tore open as he walked into the living area.

Inside the brightly decorated, homemade card—which looked like an insane craft teacher had thrown up all over it—were messages from his stepbrother and sister-in-law, his eldest niece and a proxy message from the little one. They'd even drawn on a paw print to represent the dog.

He put the card on his entertainment unit, next to his new fancy universal remote—the birthday present he'd gifted himself since his family didn't really get his love of technology. The card looked totally out of place in what Marc jokingly referred to as "the computer nerd's bachelor pad."

By the time he reached the bathroom he was itching to get out of his workout clothes. He pulled off the soaked cotton. A light ache had spread through his muscles, a sign he'd pushed himself hard today and he'd need to spend some time on the foam roller to ease out the knots.

He'd been tighter than usual the last few weeks. Stress, his trainer had said. Lack of stretching, according to the remedial masseuse. Working too hard, his buddies at the security company admonished. But he knew it wasn't any of those things.

Dissatisfaction. A lack of purpose. He'd felt it burrowing slowly under his skin, creating an incurable itch that niggled at him in the quiet portions of his day. In the dead of night. In the dark corners of his dreams.

He shook off the troubling thought and stepped under the running water, sighing as warmth seeped into him. As he lathered up, the scent of soap filled his nostrils. Perhaps it might be a good idea to put himself out there again. After all, his life couldn't be *all* work and no play.

Tomorrow.

The promise rolled around in his mind, and just like that Blondie popped back into his head, soothing all his worries away. God, she was gorgeous. Fair skin and rich golden hair, bright blue eyes. And perky breasts that seemed to often be uninhibited by a bra. This morning he'd noticed the way the pert mounds moved beneath her white tank top, the stiff little peaks of her nipples pressing forward against the fabric.

He was hard as stone just thinking about it. He wondered if those nipples would be golden like the rest of her, or would they be rosy and pink? Would she have a dusting of hair between her legs or smooth, silky skin?

He'd gone way too long without sex and now all the carnal thoughts had piled up like traffic on a highway. But a knocking sound snapped him out of the fog of arousal. He rinsed off the last of the soap suds and shut off the water. Another sharp knock rang through the apartment.

"Hang on!" he called out as he wrapped a soft gray towel around his waist, knotting it to conceal the still-raging erection he was sporting.

His wet feet skidded on the floorboards as he hurried to the door. Who on earth would be dropping by without calling first?

Grasping the knob, he pulled the door open and was greeted with the very object of his fantasies. *Blondie.*

There she was in all her golden glory, long hair tangling around her shoulders and spilling down her body. Eyes wide and blue and bright. It wasn't until he saw the wad of blood-soaked tissue in her hands that he realized something was wrong.

2

"Uh…hi," he said, his eyes darting down to her hands and widening.

Crap. This was really not how Wren had imagined their first conversation would go. Especially not after Debbie had gotten the idea of having sex into her head. But he *was* topless, and boy, oh boy, had her dreams failed to do his body justice. His muscles had muscles of their own, and the gray towel he'd knotted at his waist hid very little. A spark of arousal flared low in her belly.

"You're bleeding," he said, his eyebrows crinkled.

"Oh yes. I, uh…cut myself." A nervous laugh bubbled up in her throat but she pushed it down. No need to do anything else to convince him that she had a screw loose. "I don't have any bandages in my house and I was wondering—"

"Of course. Come in." He held the door and let it swing shut behind her. "Let me grab my first-aid kit."

"Thank you." Only then did the throbbing pain start to push through her giddy state. "I'm sorry I interrupted your shower. I should have thought to buy some bandages at the grocery store today."

But, as usual, she'd gone without a list. Or without any idea of what she needed or wanted to buy. Wren usually let the ingredients inspire her as she shopped—allowing her to make up her dinner menu on the fly—and that meant that important purchases like bandages and antiseptic lotions were often forgotten.

He pulled a small white tin down from the top of his refrigerator and opened it up. The inside was neat and tidy, like a perfect Tetris arrangement of adulthood. Band-Aids, antiseptic wipes, burn lotion, cotton balls and gauze bandages all neatly packed in a way that made her feel slightly inadequate.

"Show me." He held out his hand and she gingerly removed the wadded-up kitchen towel.

Blood immediately pooled in the slice along her palm, trailing along the crease in her skin and rushing toward the edge of her hand. She dabbed at it, but the paper was soaked through.

"Let's get that hand under some running water." He led her to the bathroom sink, her skin sparking at the comforting way he touched her arm. "You've done a number on yourself. Thankfully, it doesn't look too deep. You shouldn't need stitches."

He held her hand under the running tap, the blood washing over her fingers and staining the water pink before it swirled down the drain. In the confines of the small room—which mirrored her own except for the simple gray shower curtain that hung in place of her own chaotic rainbow version—he was incredibly close. The scent of soap on his skin filled her nostrils and made her giddy.

"Are you okay?" he asked as he pulled her hand out

from under the water to inspect the cut. "You're not going to faint, are you?"

"No." She shook her head. Thankfully, she could blame the wooziness on the blood—although the truth was it didn't bother her in the slightest. She'd never been the squeamish sort. "I'm fine."

Mr. 401 disappeared for a moment and returned with the necessary first-aid items. Within moments, she was patched up and almost as good as new.

"Thank you so much, uh…"

"Rhys." He stuck out his hand and she shook it as best she could with her injury.

"Rhys," she repeated, weighing the name in her mouth. It suited him—strong, masculine. Direct. "I'm Wren."

"The pleasure's all mine, Wren."

She inspected the expertly applied bandage. "You've done that before, haven't you?"

"I do a little downhill mountain biking. Cuts and scrapes come with the territory." When he smiled Wren felt like she was staring directly into the sun.

"Well. I'm very grateful you're so prepared."

"You make me sound like a Boy Scout." His honey-brown eyes twinkled.

Judging by the way her mouth had run dry and her heart galloped in her chest, Boy Scout was the last thing she would compare him to. Man Scout wasn't a thing… was it?

"That doesn't seem to fit you," she said, shocking herself with the flirty tone that came out of her mouth. God, if she didn't watch herself she'd be twirling her hair around her finger and batting her eyelashes like some giddy schoolgirl.

Get a grip, Livingston. He's just a man...a hunky, incredibly well-defined, thrilling man.

He chuckled, the low sound rumbling deep as thunder. It made her skin tingle. "What gives you that impression?"

"Boy Scouts don't usually have six-packs, do they?" Her tongue darted out involuntarily to moisten her lips.

What alien had taken over her body?

He didn't seem in the least bit self-conscious of his near-naked state. Wren, on the other hand, might as well have been in her birthday suit for how exposed she felt. Funny, since the naked form appeared often in her artwork...but this didn't compare with brushstrokes on a canvas. He was far too real, far too alight with sexual energy.

His eyes swept over her with a languid slowness, smoothing over her hips and breasts and hair. "No, I guess they don't."

"Can I offer you some dinner?" she blurted out. "I was making pizza when I cut myself and I'd like to thank you for coming to the rescue."

"There's no need to thank me. That's what neighbors are for, right?"

At that moment she kind of hoped neighbors were for wild, hot, no-strings sex. "Please. I'm new and I'd love to have a friend in the building."

"Well, when you put it that way." He grinned and Wren was quite sure her panties were about to melt into a puddle at her feet. "I'd love to. Give me a few minutes to change and I'll come over."

"I'll see you when you're ready." She returned his smile and headed back toward the front door, forcing herself not to bounce up and down with pent-up excitement.

It's just a dinner, you goof. A friendly, neighborly meal between two adults. It doesn't have to lead to orgasms.

But the throbbing between her legs would mark her a liar if she said she wasn't already fantasizing about it. Rhys showed her out, his broad shoulders blocking the door frame as he waited for her to make it back inside her apartment. She risked a glance behind her as she stepped inside and he was still there, the heat in his gaze unmistakable.

A tremor ran through her, excitement and fear mixing in a strange, delicious medley of emotion. The fact that her body was reacting so strongly was a good sign. After what had happened in her hometown, the very thought of sex or nakedness had filled her with guilt and shame.

But now her blood was pumping through her veins hard and fast, her heart fluttering with anticipation. Tonight, she was going to shake off the past and have a little fun.

RHYS CONSIDERED HIMSELF a logical guy. Computers were his world and binary made him feel comfortable. Even the one-two pound of running appealed to his logical side. But right now a little part of him was enjoying the thrill of a situation outside his control.

And things *could* go wrong if he slept with Wren and it didn't work out. They'd have to face each other in the hallway each day, making politely awkward small talk. There'd be guaranteed cringe-worthy moments if either one of them ever brought a date home and the other happened to see. The old Italian lady in 403 was also a huge gossip. Plus, there was a possibility that they wouldn't be compatible in the bedroom.

"Who are you kidding, man?" he muttered to himself as he whipped off his towel and proceeded to get dressed. "There's no way you have chemistry like that without it transferring to the bedroom."

And, if his still-aching erection was anything to go on, his body wholeheartedly agreed. Besides, the only way he'd ever have the chance of finding the right woman was if he actually went on dates. And dinner counted as a date…didn't it?

He pulled a fresh T-shirt over his head and fished out a pair of black boxer briefs from his bedside drawer. By the time he'd added jeans and sneakers to the mix, he'd also decided to take a bottle of wine with him.

When he knocked on her door, a thrill ran through him at the thought of seeing her again. Reality didn't disappoint. She opened the door with a flourish and a tinkling laugh. Long blond waves tumbled over one shoulder, and she'd thrown an apron over her white tank and floor-length flowy skirt.

"Welcome to my humble abode," she said, gesturing with a pair of tongs like a grand magician. "It's a little sparse at the moment. But I can assure you my pizza will make up for it."

"I have no doubt." He stepped in and took in the surroundings, placing the wine down on the kitchen counter as she grabbed two glasses.

She hadn't been kidding about it being sparse. Other than a small table with two chairs, a battered couch and an overturned cardboard box acting as a coffee table, the room was empty. He'd expected to at least see boxes with her belongings dotted around, but there wasn't a single one in sight.

"It's very…minimalist," Wren said. She poured the wine and handed him a glass, holding her own out so they could clink them together.

The wine was good, not too sweet and not too dry. The flavor danced on his tongue, and he wondered what it would taste like on her lips. Her tongue. The fantasy rushed up, tracking along his muscles until his whole body felt coiled and tight.

This is what happens when you leave it too long between drinks.

"I'm not sure how long I'll be staying," she said. "So I didn't want to waste money on getting lots of furniture."

Disappointment stabbed at him, but he brushed the feeling aside. There was no sense worrying about the future of their relationship when they hadn't even had one meal together. "Not sure if you're a fan of New York yet?"

"It's more that I'm not a fan of long-term decisions."

He cleared his throat. "Where did you move from?"

"Somewhere you've probably never heard of." She stuck the tongs in a large silver bowl filled with a colorful salad. "I'm a small-town girl."

"Living in a lonely world?" he quipped.

She grinned. "I appreciate a man who knows his Journey lyrics. Sadly, my life is far less fabulous than the song would have you believe."

"Is that why you moved to New York?" He leaned against the counter and inhaled the aromas of their dinner. Fresh basil, melting cheese, a hint of something spicy.

"I'm here for work." Her answer was carefully worded. Guarded. "But it's not a permanent position, which suits me fine."

Message received, loud and clear.

But he still wanted to get to know her better, even with her line in the sand. Perhaps "not permanent" was exactly what he needed right now. No pressure, no expectations. Like a dry run for reentering the dating world.

He could always come back to his life plan later.

"Are you a New York native?" she asked.

"I moved from Connecticut a few years ago. I've always wanted to live here, enjoy the bright lights and all that."

"Do you like it?" She whisked the salad dressing in a bowl, then plucked a teaspoon from a drawer to do a taste test.

"I do. Especially when I have such interesting neighbors."

She smiled, her cheeks flushing a vibrant shade of rose pink. "You mean clumsy neighbors who can't figure out how to slice an avocado without hurting themselves?"

"Same, same."

She moved about the kitchen with ease, her long skirt swirling around her feet with each dance-like step. There was an airiness to her, a whimsy that was so different from the serious women he was usually attracted to. She bent to open the oven and heat wafted up into the air, carrying with it the scent of her cooking.

"That smells incredible." His mouth was already watering, and he'd had some of the best pizza in all of New York. "Don't tell me you're a professional chef."

"No, just an amateur one. But I did make the base from scratch." She slid on an oven mitt and pulled out the tray containing their dinner. "I really enjoy cooking. It relaxes me…well, when I'm not cutting myself."

"Tell me that doesn't happen too often."

"Thankfully it *is* a rare occurrence." She placed the tray down on the stove and Rhys could see she was relying on her uninjured hand to hold the weight.

"Do you need a hand slicing it up?"

"No, I'll be fine. If you could take the wine to the table, that would be great."

Moments later they were seated, steaming slices of pizza resting on large white plates in front of them. But the way Wren looked at him made him hungry for something else. A sensual smile curved on her lips.

"Eat up," she said, gesturing with her hands. "It's best when it's hot."

"I like it hot," he said, picking up the slice and blowing at the steam shimmering off the pizza's surface.

"I can see that."

"Are you flirting with me?" He bit into the pizza and moaned as the hot, cheesy goodness hit his tongue.

"What if I was?" She took a bite of her slice and flicked her tongue out to catch a stray droplet of sauce. "Are you open to a little neighborly flirting?"

She folded both of her feet under her so that she sat cross-legged on top of the chair, tangling the frothy layers of her skirt around her legs. Realizing that she was still wearing her apron, she reached behind herself and untied it. As she pulled the apron over her head, her tank top rode up, revealing a slice of lightly tanned skin and smooth, flat belly.

She scrambled to tug the fabric back down, her cheeks flushing, but Rhys carried on the conversation, pretending he hadn't almost choked on his pizza. "Flirting is fine by me. In fact, I've been looking for someone to practice my flirting skills on."

"Is that so?" She reached for her wine. "Are you a little rusty?"

"That's for you to judge."

"Go on, hit me with your best pickup line." Her eyes sparkled and a smile twitched on her lips.

This was about to go downhill. Fast. Pickup lines weren't really his style. In fact, he excelled at meeting women in unconventional ways...like having them turn up at his apartment, bleeding.

He shook his head, laughing, as he took another bite out of his pizza. "I prefer a more casual approach."

She planted her fists on her waist and flapped her elbows up and down. "Buck, buck, buck."

"You did *not* just call me chicken." Damn, the girl had sass.

"Let me hear your line, then." She grinned.

"Oh, you're on." He reached his arms above his head, making a show of stretching his neck from side to side. Her eyes skated over him, wide and stormy. "I don't have a library card, but do you mind if I check you out?"

"No!" She roared, throwing her head back and letting out a burst of laughter that was belly deep and totally disarming. Totally and richly at odds with the rest of her dainty, fairylike appearance. "That's terrible."

"Are you a fruit, because honeydew you know how fine you look right now?"

She gasped. "I didn't think it could get worse—"

"Are you a parking ticket? 'Cause you've got *fine* written all over you."

"Please." She held up a hand, her shoulders heaving as laughter spilled out of her. The sound warmed him from the inside out. "Stop."

"Your body is sixty-five percent water and I'm thirsty."

He pretended to brush the dirt off his shoulders. "I could go all night."

"Okay, okay. You win." She clapped her hands together and bowed. "You are the king of the worst pickup lines I have ever had the misfortune of hearing."

"Don't say I didn't warn you."

"Fair. I promise to listen to you next time." She drained the rest of her wine and immediately topped them both up. "I'm curious now. How do you usually pick up women?"

"I'm a bit out of practice." He figured honesty was the best policy. Besides, the last thing he wanted to do was talk about the sad state of his love life right now.

"Me, too." She nodded to herself. "Looks like we're in the same boat."

Over the course of the next hour they finished the whole pizza and made a start on another bottle of wine. A delicious and languid feeling spread through him, loosening his limbs and his tongue. Maybe it was her incredible cooking, the good drink or some combination, but he couldn't remember the last time he'd felt as connected to another person as he did with Wren.

She unwound her legs and untangled her skirt, stretching her arms back and thrusting her breasts forward. His mouth watered as the fabric stretched, making it sheer enough that he could see the shadow of her nipples through the fabric.

Nope, that woman did not need to wear a bra at all.

"Thanks for sharing the pizza with me," she said, trying to sound casual. "I get a little excited when I cook and I always end up with way too much."

"I'm open to helping you deal with any leftovers that

might come up." Rhys flashed another pearly white smile and Wren wondered how many times that smile had drawn women to him. "But let me at least do the dishes."

"No way. You saved me from bleeding all over the building, trying to find bandages." She held up a hand. "Dinner was my treat. The dishes can wait."

"Well, thank you. It was delicious. You sure you're really not a chef?"

"No, I'm an artist." The words slipped out and brought with them an immediate sense of guilt. "Well, what I mean to say is that I work in a gallery."

"That's not what you said." His dark eyes scanned her face, curiosity obviously piqued. "You called yourself an artist."

Shit. She'd been so desperate to have that title for so many years that clearly the idea still floated around in her brain like a piece of flotsam waiting to trip her up. Being an artist was no longer her dream. And after she finished using her art as a cover to find out what happened to Kylie, it would be out of her life for good.

"I dabble," she said eventually, waving a hand as if to dismiss the idea.

"What sort of art?"

She swallowed against the lump in her throat. "Painting."

"I'm always fascinated by artists. I look at a painting and have no clue how the inspiration would have come to them, or how they would even know where to start." He shook his head in wonderment and it was like a knife twisting in her chest.

Years of her life had been devoted to the inspiration that had clogged her head. More years had been spent perfecting her technique, channeling her passion. Years that were now a total waste.

"What do you do?" she asked, desperate to steer the conversation away from the part of her life she wanted to leave behind.

"I'm in IT for a security company. It's like getting to solve a giant puzzle every day." He laughed. "Nerdy but true."

"People keep telling me that nerds will rule the world one day, if they don't already."

"I guess you could say that." Darkness flickered across his face before the smile returned, bringing a cheeky glint to his eye. "I don't suppose you want to show me any of your paintings? If they're half as good as your pizza, I'm betting you'll be the next Picasso."

"I don't know about that," she said, knotting her hands in her lap.

"About being Picasso or about showing me your work?"

Part of her balked at the idea of showing him her art—of showing *anyone* her art—but his face was totally earnest. His interest in her work appeared genuine, and besides, what harm could it do?

This is New York, not some tiny hick town that thinks a woman's body is a product of the devil.

"I'm no Picasso, let's be clear about that." She pushed up from her chair and motioned for him to follow. "Come on, my work space is through here."

Rhys's presence filled the air around her as they walked, his steps mirroring her own. He said nothing as she pushed open the door to her bedroom. Her mattress rested on the floor since she hadn't bought a bed frame yet. The quilt she'd been using as her duvet was draped over it, creating a white puddle of fabric around the edges of the mattress.

Early evening light filtered into the room, highlighting the stack of canvases that she'd leaned against the wall. She'd brought ten in total. Eight complete and two works in progress—though she hadn't touched a brush to them in over six months.

The canvases had been a requirement for the portfolio portion of her interview at Ainslie Ave, the gallery where she now worked as an assistant and acted as a mentee slash intern to Sean Ainslie himself.

"These are just experiments," she said, reaching for the first two in the stack. One was a vivid fall landscape and the other depicted a young student hunched over a writing desk. She'd modelled the girl on her sister, painting her long blond locks in wild swirling strokes, mimicking the fury of the student's pen scratching across paper. "They're nothing special."

"Do you really think that?" His eyes never left the paintings. They darted and scanned as though he was committing the images to memory. She watched for some sign of judgment, but he simply stared at the paintings in a way that felt fiercely intimate.

And terrifying.

"This one was from my abstract phase," she said, brushing off his question. The third canvas was a garden, but to the untrained eye the angular swipes of green paint could be anything at all.

A swamp monster, perhaps.

"And this one was a gift for my mom."

Her mother had a thing for roses and her garden back home was filled with them. Wren had painted her a small canvas for their guest room. It showed a single American Beauty bloom, just like the flower that had won her mother first place in the county fair a few years back. It'd hung on the wall until Wren had sneaked it out one night after "the incident." Nobody seemed to have noticed its absence.

"You're very talented," Rhys said, his gaze finally traveling back to her. "You've been blessed with some creative hands."

"I'm sure my parents would rather I'd been blessed with a head for numbers." The words came out stinging with truth. "My sister is going to be a doctor, so by comparison art is probably not the job they would have chosen for me."

"But you're working in a gallery, too?"

Wren dropped down onto the floor and sat cross-legged. After a moment, Rhys followed her. The rest of her canvases sat against the wall, facing away from them like a group of children who'd been sent to the naughty corner.

"Yeah, I'm an assistant for an artist who has his own gallery. I organize his appointments and manage his calendar. I also greet people who come to meet him at the gallery." She toyed with the end of her long silk skirt, twisting the fabric around on itself. "Then I get to paint in his studio and he gives me critiques and tips. Plus, I learn about how the gallery is run and get to watch him with potential buyers. Stuff like that."

"And you think you're not an artist," Rhys scoffed.

Con artist, maybe.

"It sounds weird to call myself that." She shrugged. "I guess it's a leftover doubt from my family always nagging me to get a real job and work in an office. Like you."

"Working in an office does not mean you've made it

in life." He leaned back on his forearms and surveyed the room. "Trust me."

His large form was so appealing laid out that way, a dessert for her eyes. All that sculpted muscle and sexual magnetism made her body thrum. And here he was, on her floor right in front of her. A gift for the taking.

Debs's words floated around in her head: *You won't regret it. Sex is a very natural and healthy part of life.*

She'd tried to enjoy sex with Christian, but it had been very repetitive. Her ex had only ever wanted to be on top and had complained when Wren had suggested they try other things. It was something he'd thrown back in her face when he'd discovered her secret paintings.

But something deep down told her that Rhys would be different. That *being* with Rhys would be different.

"You're looking at me very intently, Wren." His lips wrapped around her name in the most delicious way.

"I am." Tension built inside her, filling her chest and stealing her breath. "Is that a problem?"

"No problem. I was only wondering if you're planning on making a move."

Was she? Shit. She'd told herself she had time to get to know him before she acted on her attraction, and then she'd cut herself. Now they were here. And she desperately wanted to find out if her theories about him were true.

"If you're not…" His brown eyes were lit with fire. "I will."

Please. Please, please, please.

She opened her mouth to respond when a crash shattered the quiet, halting her words. The stack of paintings behind Rhys had slipped, put out of balance by her removing the heavier ones that had been holding them in place.

"I'll get them." She scrambled to her feet in an attempt to prevent him from getting there first, but she accidentally leaned on her injured hand.

"It's fine, I've got it." He reached for the paintings, his frame stilling suddenly.

Wren's face filled with heat. She didn't need to guess which painting he'd discovered.

"Wow." The word was so filled with shock that it made her stomach twist into a knot. "This is…"

"I wasn't going to show you that one." She walked over to the pile and started replacing them against the wall, flames licking her cheeks.

He held the painting in his hand—the one that had been the cause of her troubles back home and, most ironically, the one she secretly thought of as her best. It was of a woman, her legs open and her head thrown back in ecstasy. Eyes closed. Lips slack.

The shades of pink and red and brown blended together, raw and earthy. It was intensely sexual, so much so that Wren wasn't sure how she'd painted it. At the time her brush had moved as if of its own accord. The painting wasn't hers; it belonged to someone else. To some*thing* else.

"Please give it to me." She held out her hand, hating the way her voice trembled when it should have sounded cool and unaffected. But those were two things that her tender heart had never been able to master.

She was *always* affected by what other people thought.

"Please," she demanded, this time louder.

Rhys handed her the painting, a strange look on his face. It wasn't outright disgust, as had been Christian's expression. But she couldn't handle even the mildest form of judgment right now. Not about this.

The only reason she'd even brought the damn thing with her was because Kylie had mentioned that Sean Ainslie had a thing for nude portraits.

Now the damn thing was humiliating her again.

"I think you should go," she said, fighting back the wave of shame as memories assaulted her.

You're depraved, Christian had said when he'd discovered this painting along with the twelve others in the collection. All nudes, all women. *You're a sexual deviant and you're using me as a cover.*

It wasn't true. She had simply been fascinated by the idea of female sexuality. Enamored by it from an artistic standpoint…not that anyone in her damned hometown would understand that. All they had seen were things that should be hidden away.

"Wren," he started. "There's nothing to be ashamed of."

"I'm not ashamed," she lied. "I would just prefer it if you left now. Please."

He hovered for a moment, his eyes, which had darkened to almost black, flicking between her and the canvas that she held tight to her chest. Protecting herself or the painting, she wasn't sure.

"For what it's worth, I think your paintings are incredible," he said, shoving his hands into his pockets. "Thanks again for dinner."

"You're welcome." Her voice was a whisper as he walked out of the room, leaving her alone to ponder why the fates had decided yet again to use her art to humiliate her.

"Maybe you should take a hint," she muttered to herself as she placed the remaining paintings back where they belonged. "Listen to your parents and get a real job."

She would. Just as soon as she figured out what had happened to Kylie, she would head home and enter the real world.

3

WREN SAT BEHIND the sleek chrome-and-marble desk that crowned the entrance to the Ainslie Ave gallery. Her boss was expecting a potential client for a private viewing, so he was locked away in his studio preparing, which left her with a few precious moments of solitude to do some digging.

Hopefully, the chance to snoop would not only yield some valuable information but also help her to keep her mind off Rhys. And how he probably thought she was a nut job after the way she'd ordered him out of her apartment last night.

She cringed. The whole evening had been going so well. They'd had a great rapport and she'd gotten definite vibes of interest from him. Heated glances, an invitation to make a move. Then she'd blown it.

"Rookie move, Livingston," she muttered to herself as she clicked out of Sean's calendar. "You don't think before you act."

It was a criticism that had been handed to her over and over by her parents. Most of the time it followed, "Why can't you be more responsible, like your sister?" Wren had never been too good at plotting out her moves before she made them. Often guided by impulse, she'd landed herself in hot water on a few occasions and had earned herself a bit of a reputation—unfairly, in her opinion— for being a wild girl.

She wasn't wild. Irresponsible, perhaps. Spontaneous, definitely. But certainly not wild in the sense that they meant it back home.

Not that anyone believed her.

Shaking off the well-worn thoughts, she forced herself to focus on the task at hand. Her self-loathing could wait. She'd been working here for exactly three weeks now and all her preliminary searches had turned up zilch. Well, unless you counted a snarky online review of an exhibition Sean had run two years ago…which she didn't.

Sliding down from her stool, she padded quietly across the showroom floor. The place was silent save for the swish of her skirt against the polished boards. The other two interns, with whom she shared reception duties and a cramped studio space, were painting today. She'd gotten to know them quite well in the last few weeks—thanks to the assistance of her amazing chocolate brownies— although she could tell both girls believed Sean Ainslie was a god among men.

The paintings in the showroom had been switched around this morning after Sean's conversation with the client. He'd since selected a shortlist of works that he thought would suit the client's needs. The rest of the paintings were locked away in some specially designed climate-controlled room to which Wren had not yet gained access.

Sean Ainslie came from money; she knew that for sure. His wealth wasn't due to his art, although he'd had moderate success with a collection of paintings depicting the burned-out carcass of the iconic New York yellow cab. Yet the paintings he had ready for viewing were entirely different in feel and style.

Wren studied a smaller canvas, which showed an ice-cream cone melting in the sun. The painting had a slight cubism feel to it, the shapes on the waffle cone exaggerated and angular. Sharp. The vibrant colors seemed at odds with Sean's darker, grittier pieces.

"Why were you drawn to that one?" Sean's voice echoed against the high ceilings and bounced around, causing Wren to jump.

"It's different from your other works." Wren pressed a hand to her chest and felt her heart beat wildly beneath her skin. Sean unnerved her, especially his ability to sneak up on her out of nowhere. "I was wondering what inspired it."

"I used to visit Coney Island with my grandfather when I was a kid." He came up behind her and stood close. Too close. "Everything about that place was so… plastic. It felt unreal to me, even back then. Like it was something I'd made up in my head instead of being a real place."

The scent of stale cigarette on his breath made Wren's stomach churn. She tried to subtly put some distance between them by pretending to look more closely at the painting. "I've never been there."

"Don't bother. It's a cesspool."

"Right." She nodded.

"Have you got the coffee on?"

"Yes." Taking the opportunity, she stepped away from him and returned to her post at the front of the showroom. "I've also put out the croissants. Mr. Wagner should be here in five minutes. Would you like me to stay in the room in case you need anything?"

Please say no, please say no, please say no.

Sean's thin lips pressed into a line as he considered her question. The scar on his left cheek seemed to twitch as the muscle behind it moved. "No, leave Mr. Wagner to me. The last thing I want is him getting distracted by a beautiful young woman."

Wren forced her expression to stay neutral, despite her lip wanting to curl at the sleazy way he was looking at her. "Very well."

"Feel free to get some work done in the studio, but don't go home. I'll need you to clean up once Mr. Wagner has gone."

"Of course."

She retreated before Sean could make any more requests…or comments about her appearance. He seemed to do that on a daily basis. Wren certainly wasn't averse to compliments, but her skin always seemed to crawl whenever he was around.

The other interns—a blonde named Aimee and a girl with a Southern accent named Lola—were painting in relative silence in the studio. Their stations were crowded with paints and tools, like chaotic rainbows of creativity. Her section, in stark comparison, was spotlessly clean.

If only her mother could see that for once she had the cleanest workstation in the room.

Sadly, this wasn't due to a newfound love of tidiness… but more because her Muse had refused to show up. She'd taken on more reception duties to avoid her creative block, but Sean would expect her to produce something eventually. After all, she should be having the time of her life with an opportunity so many other artists would kill for.

Supposedly, anyway.

"Looks like it's just you and me, old friend." Wren stood in front of the canvas, which was mostly blank except for an angry-looking smudge in one corner. She laughed to herself in the quiet room, the sound rough and insincere. "And with friends like these, who needs enemies?"

Neither Aimee nor Lola glanced in her direction. But before Wren had a chance to pick up a brush, the sound of talking floated down from the showroom. Sean's client had arrived, which meant he would be occupied for some time. That gave her a window of opportunity to check out the storage room and some of the other rooms at the back of the gallery where she didn't normally go.

Tiptoeing out into the corridor, she listened to make sure that no one was coming her way. The storage room was at the very end of the building—which had once been a mechanic's workshop that had lain abandoned for several years until Sean had purchased it. The storage room had been tacked on to the structure and fitted with a keypad to limit entry. Wren hadn't yet been able to come up with an excuse that would allow her to request access from Sean.

She stared helplessly at the blinking keypad. It seemed strange to lock up a storage room so tightly. Even if it housed valuable paintings, why were the interns kept out? It didn't make sense. Wren had worked in a small gallery a few towns over from Charity Springs. Sure, small towns were different from the Big Smoke, but she'd always had access to the gallery's stock.

What had she been thinking turning up here without

a plan? For the first time in three weeks, Wren felt the stupidity of her decision weigh on her. A naive part of her had assumed it would be easy to show up here, figure out what had happened and run back home, evidence in hand. Ready to reassure her friend that she would have justice, after all.

"That's because you don't think before you act," she muttered to herself. Again.

"Wren?" A female voice caught her attention. "Are you free? I have a question."

Wren spun to find Aimee peering out of the studio, her fair brows wrinkled. "What's wrong, Aimee?"

"I need to put a note into the shared calendar about my day off this week and I couldn't get in. Then I tried to reset the password and now I've locked us all out." She threw her hands up in the air. "I don't know why computers hate me so much."

Wren tried not to roll her eyes. In the three weeks she'd been working at Ainslie Ave, Aimee had managed to lock herself out of the computer system at least four times. Clumsy fingers, she'd claimed, but Wren found that hard to believe considering the delicate and intricate portraits she painted.

"Can you help me?" the other woman pleaded. "I don't want to disturb Sean again. He got very frustrated last time."

"Sure." Wren headed back into the studio and took a seat on the stool in front of the old laptop that served as their shared work computer.

Within minutes she'd located the problem—Aimee had made a spelling error when she'd created her new password, which explained why she hadn't been able to use it to log in after the reset.

"Okay, that should do it." Wren clicked over to their email program. "I've reset it again and tested that it works. I'll leave a note on the desktop with the password this time so you don't forget it."

"Thanks." Aimee had the decency to look mildly sheepish.

Wren was about to move away from the computer when she noticed something strange about the email inbox. A ton of unread emails had banked up from contacts she'd never seen before. Normally, the inbox the three women shared was filled with general requests from the website's contact form. There might be the occasional email requesting information or dates of shows, but otherwise they didn't get many direct emails from clients.

"Are you logged in to Sean's email account?" Wren asked, looking up suddenly.

Aimee cringed. "Yes, but please don't tell him. I needed to, uh…delete an email." She fiddled with the end of her paint-splattered tank top, the chipped pink nail polish on her fingers glinting like shards of broken glass in the afternoon sun that streamed in from a large window beside them.

"How did you get into his account?" Wren could hardly believe Aimee was the password-cracking type.

"He keeps it written down." She averted her gaze and spoke softly so that Lola couldn't hear them. "Please don't say anything."

Wren knew for a fact that his passwords weren't written down anywhere in the studio…after all, she'd looked. Which meant that Aimee had been places that Wren hadn't, and from the expression on her face she wasn't too comfortable sharing that information.

"I won't, but I don't think it's a good idea to be logging in to his email account from our shared computer. You might get someone in trouble," she admonished, feeling immediately hypocritical because she knew exactly how she was going to exploit this opportunity.

"You're right," Aimee said, knotting her hands in front of her. "I'm sorry. I don't want to get anyone in trouble."

"I won't say anything." Wren turned the laptop back to herself. "And I'll log out so I can check on the shared inbox and make sure we haven't missed anything. You'd better get back to your painting in case he comes in."

"Thank you."

Perhaps it made Wren a horrible person to be admonishing Aimee while planning to use her lapse in judgment to scan through Sean's emails. But Wren had learned a thing or two about morals in the last six months—they were not as black-and-white as she'd been led to believe. For example, in Christian's mind it had been perfectly okay for him to make up stories about her because he felt she was a bad person for hiding her "depravity."

Besides, she wasn't hurting Aimee. She was simply making use of a happy accident to help her friend.

There was nothing suspicious in his emails. Time for plan B. Her nails clicked quietly against the keys of the laptop as she searched for the passcode to the storage room. Nothing. But she did manage to find his birthday, address and home phone number, which gave her something to work with. Wren wasn't a master spy by any stretch, but she *had* sat in on an internet security session at the community center back home during one of her volunteering stints. At the time she'd thought it was boring as hell, but some of the stats had stuck with her. Like how the majority of people use their birthdays as pin codes for ATMs and online banking. Perhaps that extended to locked rooms, as well.

Taking a second to check that no one was watching her, she logged out of Sean's email and pocketed the note she'd scribbled with his details. Tonight, after everyone had left, she'd "accidentally" forget to set the alarm so she could come back and have a crack at the storage room lock without leaving a trail.

RHYS WASN'T THE kind of guy who ever had trouble sleeping. He pushed his body hard at the gym and he pushed his mind hard at work each day. Those things combined meant he was usually out the moment his head hit the pillow.

But not for the last three nights.

Stifling a yawn, he rubbed at his eyes and reached for the coffee on his desk. The nighttime hours had been ticking past slowly while Rhys's eyes remained open in the darkness. All he could picture were flashes of Wren and her painting. Of the sexual energy mixed with her embarrassment.

He hadn't seen hide nor hair of her since that night… but that didn't dull the vivid memory.

The painting had taken him aback. Not because he thought there was anything wrong with it—far from it. But he'd been shocked by how strongly his body had reacted to the desire and curiosity and abandonment in her work. Art was not his thing—numbers and data were. But she'd invoked a kind of visceral reaction that was totally foreign.

And then she'd kicked him out.

He wasn't sure what to make of it. But one thing he

did know for certain was that he wanted to see her again, despite understanding that she wasn't planning to stay.

"Boss?" Quinn Dellinger poked her head into his office, her mass of dyed pink hair almost blindingly bright under the office lighting. "You got a sec?"

"Sure, sure." He motioned for her to take a seat as he shoved thoughts of Wren from his mind. Work was his priority right now, not women. Not one woman, no matter how tempting. "What's going on?"

Quinn's chunky combat boots clomped on the floor. For a woman so petite she made a lot of noise. "I've been assigned a case but I need to do a site visit and none of the other guys are free to come with me."

As a newly appointed junior security consultant, Quinn wasn't yet cleared to do site visits on her own. She had another few months of shadowing the more experienced consultants before that could happen.

"I'm ready," she added. "I can do it. I just need you to sign off."

"You're familiar with the policy, Quinn. Three months of supervision before you can fly solo."

Her button nose wrinkled, causing the clear stud there to glint in the afternoon sunlight. "And it's worth upsetting the client for some stupid policy?"

"It's not a stupid policy. We have it for a reason."

He didn't need to repeat the story; *everyone* at Cobalt & Dane Security was well aware of what had happened when they'd sent a rookie in alone. One bad incident was all it took to make sure that new security consultants had the proper training and supervision so that they didn't lose anyone else.

"I know how capable you are, Quinn. I wouldn't have promoted you if I didn't believe in your skills." Rhys reached for his coffee and swigged, praying the caffeine would soon work its magic. "But that doesn't mean I'm going to bend the rules for you."

She rolled her eyes but a smile twitched on her lips. "You *never* bend the rules. For anything."

"Tough but fair, you know the drill," he said.

"Yeah, yeah." She folded her arms across the front of her black skull-and-crossbones T-shirt. "So what should we do about the client, then? He said he wants us there today but everyone else is busy."

"I thought Owen was in the office today."

She shook her head. "He got an emergency call out to that private client we signed—the crazy stockbroker guy. He's paranoid. I told Owen as much."

"It comes with the territory. Doesn't mean we can ignore the client's needs." Rhys tapped his fingers against the surface of his desk. "And Jin is still out sick?"

"Yep. Aiden's around but he's scheduled to do a visit to the data warehouse with Logan." Quinn's cheeks colored slightly despite the neutral expression on her face. She and Aiden had only told the team they were dating a few weeks back, and every time his name came up in conversation she blushed like a schoolgirl.

Rhys thought it was cute, but Quinn would probably throw something at him for saying so. "Okay, well, I guess it'll have to be me, then."

Perhaps a trip away from the office would do him good. He'd been staring at the same email for the last ten minutes and his lack of progress was starting to grate on his nerves. Fresh air and something to focus on might help him to get into the zone again.

"You never do site visits." Quinn cocked her head. "Ever."

"You seem to think I never do a lot of things."

God, did everyone really believe he was that dull? Sure, he liked to follow the rules. He was a "by the book" kind of guy. What was so bad about that?

She shrugged, seemingly unaware of the questions her words had stirred. "Whatever works. I'd rather get out there today and keep this guy onside. He sounds like a bit of a control freak."

"Let's keep our insults about the client to a minimum, shall we?" Rhys pushed up from his chair and stuck his phone into his back pocket.

"Sure thing, boss. Whatever you say." Quinn grinned at him as they fell into step.

After a quick pause at her desk so she could collect her things and confirm with the client that they would now be coming to complete the site visit, they were off.

"This will be fun. We haven't had an excursion together in ages." Quinn had a spring in her step as they walked through the office.

"That's because you're annoying."

He didn't mean it, but he and Quinn had that kind of relationship. There were no filters, no walking on eggshells. She was one of the first people he'd hired when he'd started as IT manager four years ago. They'd developed a deep mutual respect. She was whip smart and loyal to the bone, two qualities that were sorely lacking in the world.

"*I'm* annoying?" She pressed her hand to her chest and he noticed a small, heart-shaped ring on her finger. "Those are mighty words coming from Mr. Spreadsheet himself."

He ignored the dig. "What's with the ring? I've never seen you wear anything that didn't have a skull on it."

Her cheeks turned hot pink. "It was a gift."

"Are you engaged?"

"No." She laughed as if that were a ridiculous notion, but her voice sounded tight and a little strange. "It's just a ring."

"A ring from your boyfriend." He nudged her with his elbow and she immediately swatted him. "Hey, I'm not judging. I'm happy you've found someone who puts up with you."

"He's man enough to handle me." Her expression turned serious as they entered the elevator. "I know you two didn't get off on the right foot, but he's it for me. I love him."

Rhys had been forced to hire Aiden because he was friends with the boss, Logan Dane. Given Rhys's feelings about hard work and the need to prove oneself, it hadn't been a great start to their working relationship.

"You're getting all mushy on me, Dellinger," he joked.

"It's true. He's a good guy, Rhys. I want you to respect him."

Rhys didn't point out that respect had to be earned instead of given out like candy. But Quinn was practically family to him, so he would keep his feelings to himself and take the high road. He *always* took the high road.

"I do respect him. He's on my team now so I'll treat him the same as I treat any other employee."

She grinned. "Tough, but fair."

"That's my motto."

"I appreciate it." She laid a hand on his arm, the pink stone in her ring glimmering. "Honestly."

He cleared his throat. "For what it's worth, you deserve to be happy."

"So do you, boss. Why don't you ever seem to have any ladies hanging around?"

Probably because Rhys kept his work life and his love life totally separate. He'd never believed in mixing the two, though he accepted that not everyone agreed with him on that.

But that didn't mean he could avoid the little stabs of envy he got watching his friends pair up and find happiness. Maybe it was old-fashioned, but he wanted that stability. He wanted a woman to come home to, wake up next to. To make him feel like he was valued. Needed.

"This is not appropriate conversation for a manager and his employee," he said, reminding himself that the goal right now was to have fun with a woman and *not* worry about the future.

"Stick-in-the-mud," she grumbled.

She might be right, but right now Rhys didn't have anything that he wanted to share. Especially not with being so occupied by Wren and her painting. His whole body hummed as she drifted back into his mind. There was no way he'd be able to forget what he'd seen, so he'd just have to stage a meeting with her to clear the air. And maybe fulfill a few fantasies...

4

"YOU'RE AVOIDING SOMETHING, WREN." Sean Ainslie's voice cut into Wren's thought process.

Her brush hovered over the same patch of blank canvas that she'd been attempting to start work on for the last half hour.

"Avoiding something?" She put the brush down onto her workstation and looked up. "What makes you say that?"

His eyes swept over the lackluster canvas. A few strokes of color decorated one of the bottom corners but it was clear she had no direction. She hadn't sketched anything out, hadn't planned what the painting would look like. Hell, she couldn't even legitimately claim that she was too swept away by her Muse to do any of the preparatory work.

She had nothing, and as a result, the painting *was* nothing.

Oh, it's something all right. It's a hot freaking mess, is what it is.

"I saw so much inspiration in your portfolio, Wren. So much…" His hands fluttered in the air in front of him.

"Passion. Creativity. Your paintings were bold and vibrant. This…" His hands dropped down to his sides. "I don't know what this is. Do you?"

"I'm a little blocked," she admitted.

Every time she tried to touch the paintbrush to the canvas she pictured Rhys's expression when he'd looked at *that* painting. The memory filled her with a strange mélange of excitement and shame, anticipation and disgust. Part of her wished that she'd let him stay. If for nothing more than to see where they would have ended up. Visions of his deep brown skin and warm eyes filled her mind.

"Just paint whatever pops into your head right now." Sean touched her shoulder and she jumped, startled as she reached for her brush almost involuntarily. "Whatever image is in your mind now, paint it. I want you to get over this hurdle, Wren."

Biting down on her lip she shut her eyes and let the memory of Rhys gazing at the painting wash over her. His full lips, the wicked way they'd parted as his eyes had widened. The slight flare of his nostrils.

She started mixing paint as she let her mind wander. His pupils had grown as he'd looked at her canvas, his breath stalling in his throat. Her life had contained few moments as electric as that, as intensely intimate and vulnerable. Wasn't that the purpose of art? Laying yourself bare?

Being open and receptive?

But that's how she'd been hurt before. With her heart so open and unprotected, it was ripe for the picking. Her fingers tightened around her brush as she stopped midstroke. The faint sketch of a man's face—the high points of his cheeks, the rough contours of his lips and the strong angle of his jaw—filled the canvas.

People can only hurt you when you let them. So don't give them the opportunity.

Her hand hovered again, the moment lost like steam into air. Fear had crept back in and chased inspiration away. Sighing, she threw the brush down into the palette, flicking sienna paint across the carefully mixed palette of earthy flesh tones.

It was useless. *She* was useless.

Sean opened his mouth to say something but they were interrupted when Lola poked her head into the room. "Sean? I've got the security people from Cobalt & Dane here to see you."

"Tell them I'll be out momentarily," he said. As Lola disappeared he turned back to Wren. "I want to see a complete painting next week. The whole point of you being here is to work on improving your art. I can't help you with that if you don't produce anything."

"I understand."

"If you're not able to do that I'll have to find another intern. It's not fair for you to take a valuable position in my program if you're not going to do the work. There are plenty of other artists who would eagerly step into your place."

The words stung but she kept her face neutral. "I'll do better, I promise."

When Sean left the room, Aimee turned from her station and offered a sympathetic smile. "It's not easy to be creative on demand, is it?"

The genuine empathy caused moisture to rush to Wren's eyes, but she blinked the tears away. She wasn't the kind of girl to let her pain show; she locked it all away where no one could see how much she allowed other people's words to cut her.

"No," she admitted. "It's not."

"You just have to give yourself permission to be crap," Aimee said.

"That flies in the face of every piece of advice I've ever received." Wren frowned at her canvas as she picked up her brush.

Her whole life she'd told herself she needed to be incredible, that she needed to be "the best." That's why it'd hurt so bad when Kylie had initially been chosen over her to gain a place in Ainslie's internship.

If she couldn't be the best, then her parents would never consider her art as anything but a hobby. But if her talent was honed and she pushed herself hard, they might believe in her.

Giving herself permission to be crap was laughable.

"Hear me out." Aimee put her brush down and flicked her long blond ponytail over one shoulder. "I can almost guarantee you're psyching yourself out of this painting. You keep thinking that no matter what you do it'll never be enough, right?"

"Well, not exactly…"

"But close enough?"

Wren huffed. "Maybe."

"So give yourself permission to paint something no matter how crappy it is. Better at this point to have a crappy painting than no painting at all." She folded her arms over her apron and smiled with an air of smugness. "Trust me, it'll get the creativity flowing again."

Maybe she had a point. If Wren failed Sean's ultimatum, it would put a swift end to her mission. Better to give him a mediocre product rather than a blank canvas.

He might kick her out of the internship anyway, but she could still have a chance. Whereas if she continued on the path she was on, she'd *definitely* be out.

Wren sucked in a breath and touched her brush to a shade of burnt orange. Perhaps painting Rhys would help get him out of her head. Then she could kill two birds with one painting.

RHYS FOUND HIMSELF tuning out as the client went on a diatribe about how underappreciated artists were. Judging by Quinn's glazed-over eyes, she was struggling to pay attention, as well.

"Why don't we talk through the security incidents you mentioned over the phone, Mr. Ainslie?" Quinn suggested tactfully. "You said there was some unauthorized access to your storage room…?"

"Right." Sean Ainslie narrowed his dark brows and interlaced his fingers. "I have a storage room where I keep all the paintings that aren't on display. They're very valuable, you see."

"Of course." Quinn nodded, one hand fiddling with the pink ends of her braid. "What alerted you to the break-in?"

"The thief didn't actually get into the room. The incorrect pin code was entered three times and I have my system set up to alert me when that happens. I had to reset it the following day. I questioned the staff here but no one has owned up to it."

"So was anything stolen?"

"No. Nothing. But I think the culprit may try again, so I'd like to take some preventative measures. I've been a customer of Cobalt & Dane for quite a few years now, but I've never had an incident this severe before."

"I assume you'll be happy to give us access to your security-camera footage," Rhys said.

Sean looked sheepish for a moment. "There isn't any."

"You don't have security cameras?" Rhys resisted the urge to raise a brow. "Or the footage isn't accessible?"

"There are no cameras."

Rhys's suspicions were instantly roused. What kind of person would store a bunch of valuable paintings in a room with a high-tech locking system and then not have security cameras? It didn't make sense.

"Hasn't someone from Cobalt & Dane advised you that a monitoring system for the gallery would be a good idea?"

"I don't like the idea of having cameras on my employees," he explained. "I trust these girls, and the idea of having cameras on them felt a bit *1984*."

Quinn cast a glance to Rhys, which confirmed that she also wasn't buying his story. "Okay," she said slowly. "You also mentioned an email breach…?"

"I was looking for an email in my inbox the other day but I found it in the deleted folder. I definitely didn't delete it. I think someone has been accessing my emails, as well."

"Quinn can have a look through the email security logs and see if there's any strange activity," Rhys said. "Do you have any idea what this person might be after?"

"Not a clue." Sean shook his head, but there was a guardedness to his expression that didn't seem to match his words. The guy was hiding something; Rhys was sure of it. "All my paintings are valuable, but there isn't one that's worth significantly more than the others."

"Try to think if there's anything in particular a thief might want. It might not be a painting. It could be information. We strongly recommend that you install cameras. It will be hard for us to assist you in keeping this place secure if there isn't anything for us to monitor. In the meantime, it might be worthwhile for us to have a chat with your employees. I understand you've already talked to them, but it would be good for us to go over anything that they might have seen or heard."

"Of course." Sean motioned for them to follow him back out into the gallery.

"You can take the lead in talking to the staff," Rhys said to Quinn as their footsteps echoed through the spacious gallery showroom. "If you get stuck I'll jump in."

"Great." Quinn nodded, lowering her voice as they let Sean walk ahead. "We should debrief when we get back to the office."

"Agreed."

After spending a few minutes with a dark-haired woman named Lola, who appeared genuinely shocked that anything was amiss, they headed past Sean's office to the studio.

"My other two interns are in here," Sean said as he rounded a corner into an airy space lit with streaming natural sunlight. "Aimee and Wren, this is Rhys and Quinn. They're here to ask a few questions and I expect you both to give them whatever they need."

Rhys's chest clenched when he caught sight of Wren, her golden-blond hair piled messily on top of her head and a streak of dark orange paint on her cheek contrasting against her fair skin.

What a coincidence.

Her blue eyes widened in mild panic as her lips formed an O shape. No sound came out.

"I need to make a phone call," Sean said. "I trust you two will be fine to talk with the girls?"

"Quinn, why don't you talk with Aimee in one of the other rooms and I'll stay in here with Wren," Rhys said, his voice smooth and unflustered. He knew exactly how to sound in charge—the product of years of faking it until he made it.

"Sure thing, boss." Quinn introduced herself to the other intern and they left him alone with Wren a minute later. An easel and canvas partially obscured his view of her.

"Well, this is quite a surprise," Rhys said, keeping his distance. The last thing he wanted to do was spook her, especially given how their last encounter had ended.

"You're telling me," she said, her hands knotting in front of her. She wore a long flowing dress colored with swirls of pale blue and purple. The thin straps left plenty of skin visible. A simple silver chain held a piece of roughly cut blue stone just below her bust. "What are you doing here?"

"We're looking into a few security concerns for your boss."

"Oh?" Her tone and expression gave nothing away.

"There was a failed attempt to access the storage room as well as suspected email hacking." He leaned against the wall and folded his arms across his chest.

"I don't know anything about that." The response was too automatic. Defensive.

"That's okay. We're going to be taking some preventative measure to ensure it doesn't happen again." He inched closer and noticed her body tense up. "Is it okay if we talk? I can bring Quinn in, if that would make you more comfortable."

"No, that's fine."

"What are you working on?" He thought he'd start with something easy, something nonthreatening. But the second he took a step forward she visibly pulled back, her body language screaming at him not to come closer.

Maybe he'd misread the situation when they had had dinner together.

"It's no good."

"I've seen your work, Wren. I'm sure it's incredible." God, who had treated her so badly that she thought so lowly of herself? Of her work?

"You seem to have a lot of blind faith in my abilities," she said, her hands wringing in her lap.

"Well, I'm no expert but I know what I like." He inched closer.

"It's not finished," she said with a note of resignation. Her eyes lowered to her lap and he peered around the edge of the canvas.

The image struck him. It wasn't more than a collection of rough strokes, lacking the depth and shading that she'd no doubt add later on. But the image was unmistakable. He recognized his own deep brown eyes and broad nose, the warm tone of his skin and the heavy shadow along his jaw.

Words eluded him.

"You weren't supposed to see this," she said, pushing up from her stool.

"That's the second time you've said that to me." He tore his eyes away from his own image.

"I don't know which one was more embarrassing," she admitted, folding her arms across her chest. "But in any case, you're not here to discuss my work. So ask me what you need to ask me."

"Have you noticed anything strange going on in the studio? Any people hanging around that seem suspicious?"

She shook her head. "No, I don't think so."

"Any odd phone calls?"

"Not that I can recall."

"Have either of the other girls been acting strange? Asking questions about the storage room or security?"

Her delicate shoulders lifted into a shrug. "Well, they wouldn't ask me those questions because I don't have any more access than they do. We all share an email account and work out of this room, and we take turns at the front desk and help Sean organize his schedule."

"So no one is in charge?"

"Just Sean. There's no hierarchy among us interns."

Wren had a good poker face, he'd give her that. He couldn't be sure if she was telling the truth or hiding something, since her initial defensiveness seemed mostly related to the painting.

Excitement stirred inside him. Imagining her sitting at this very stool, her mind on him as she swept her brush over the canvas, caused a tight ache in his chest. Why would she choose him?

Drawing a deep breath, he shoved the questions aside. Right now he was on company time, so those curiosities would have to wait until later. He dug a card out of his jacket pocket. "Here's my number. If you see anything out of the ordinary, give me a call."

"Sure." She took the card and turned it over in her hands. "I'll do that."

Silence hung in the air but he couldn't tear himself away from her. Not yet. Not when she'd been the ghost in his mind for the last few days. The faint sound of

Quinn's voice floated into the room. She was still questioning the other intern.

"I haven't seen you around much." He jammed his hands into the pockets of his suit pants.

Her lips lifted into a rueful smile. "That's because I've been avoiding you."

"Honest. I like that."

"Well, cat's out of the bag now, isn't it? You're a smart man. I wouldn't try to pull one over on you." Her fingers toyed with her necklace, causing the blue stone to shift and catch the light. It was roughly cut, raw and natural in its beauty. Like her.

"I felt like we had unfinished business after the other night," he said. That was putting it mildly.

"That's what I've been avoiding."

So maybe he *hadn't* misread the signals. "Why?"

"I had a rough time back home and I came here to get away from it all. I'm still…wounded," she said carefully, her eyes focused on the window that looked out into the alley behind the building. "I don't want to get hurt again."

"I guess it's a good thing I'm not planning on hurting anyone. Well, other than the bad guys."

"Of course." A smile crossed her lips but it didn't quite come up to her eyes. "Very noble of you."

He cleared his throat. "If you feel like company tonight, I have a very comfortable couch and I'm not a terrible cook, if I do say so myself."

It was probably wrong for him to engage with her outside the boundaries of the job, but hell, they were neighbors. This conversation could have happened anywhere. And besides, this was Quinn's assignment, and other than supervising her site visits, she'd be doing the investigative portion. So it wasn't like there was a conflict of interest.

Wren's hesitation thickened the air around them. "A comfortable couch?"

"Yeah, that thing people sit on while they watch TV? It's long and has cushions—"

She swatted him and laughed. "I know what a couch is."

"So come and hang out on mine. We'll eat, have a drink… We don't have to address the unfinished business if you don't want."

The furrow of her fair brows tugged at his heart. "Why are you being so nice to me?"

"You don't know anyone in the city, as you said the other night." He shrugged. "I thought you might like the company."

"Another noble gesture."

"And my apartment is fully furnished, so there's that."

She tried to purse her lips but a grin broke through. "Are you judging the state of my apartment, Rhys?"

"Not at all."

"I'm going for the bohemian-chic look," she said unconvincingly. "It's all the rage."

"Is it?"

Her tinkling laugh echoed against the high, white ceilings and the sound barreled through him. Damn, that sound could put him on cloud nine. "No idea. I'm just making things up as I go."

"That's all any of us can do."

At that moment Quinn stuck her head into the room. "Ready to go, boss?"

He stepped away from Wren, suddenly aware of how they'd gravitated toward one another. The space had shrunk between them until her shoulder was mere inches from his. She seemed to have that effect on him.

"Yes, let's make a move. I'll meet you out front," he said. When Quinn retreated, he turned back to Wren. "If you decide to come over, I usually have dinner around seven."

He actually had dinner precisely at seven every night, but he suspected that would sound a little type A if he said it aloud.

"I'll keep that in mind." She rolled her bottom lip between her teeth and a light flush crept over her cheeks.

As he walked out of the studio, he forced himself to keep his eyes forward. If she came over, great. If not, well, he wouldn't push it. But his body was already coiled tight with the thought that she might want to pick up where they'd left off.

He'd just have to be careful to keep a clear demarcation between his work and his extracurricular activities. But it wouldn't be an issue—he had no reason to suspect Wren was involved in the security breach. She had her own paintings—what could she possibly need with Sean Ainslie's?

5

WREN HAD BEEN on edge ever since Rhys had shown up at work. Not just because he'd appeared as if the images in her head had come to life, but because he was there hunting for things *she'd* done. Naively, she'd assumed that when her attempt to get into the storage room had failed her boss would be none the wiser.

Wrong. Now he'd hired a security company to come in and investigate, which would no doubt throttle her ability to play detective.

So why was she standing at Rhys's door, her hand poised to knock?

"Because you're a glutton for punishment, that's why," she muttered. "You don't know when to back away."

Her logical side—she *did* have one, though it was the runt of the litter—said it would be better to keep in contact with Rhys so she could stay abreast of his company's investigation. Her emotional side thought that sounded manipulative, and she supposed it was. But the fact that Sean had involved a security firm meant he was extremely serious about protecting his privacy, and that made her even more suspicious of him.

So she'd have to forcibly ignore her guilt about lying to Rhys. She didn't like being dishonest, but she wasn't about to give up on finding justice for Kylie.

"You're doing it for her." She stared at the gold-plated numbers on Rhys's door for a moment longer before she knocked. "Kylie would do the same for you."

Footsteps sounded inside and then Rhys swung the door open. Wren's knees almost buckled at the dazzling smile he gifted her. Paired with the fitted black T-shirt that stretched across his broad chest and the half apron accentuating his trim waist, it was a killer combination.

"Couldn't resist my offer?" He held the door open and motioned for her to enter.

"I couldn't resist the offer of a comfy couch. I think mine was home to a family of raccoons before I got here."

"If that's what brought you here, I'll take it."

Wren had been in Rhys's apartment before, but she'd been more focused on her bleeding hand and his half-naked state the last time she was here. Now she had the opportunity to take in his space.

It was tidy to a fault, not a single cushion out of order. Next to the big-screen TV, he'd hung a shelf that was lined with books arranged by height. A set of hand weights rested in a rack near the window. They, too, were arranged by size. On top of the solid coffee table was a fancy-looking remote.

"You may be the tidiest person I have ever met," she said, gazing around the apartment and feeling slightly inadequate. "Seriously, I want to fling some paint across your floor just to mess things up."

"A clean space is a clean mind," Rhys replied as he headed back to the kitchen. "I can't think if there's too much clutter. Besides, it doesn't take much effort to keep something clean. I have a system in place."

"A system?"

"Yeah, a routine, you might call it."

"Stop. This conversation is becoming way too adult for me." She leaned against the kitchen counter as he gathered up a handful of chopped onions and tossed them into a pan on the stove.

"I guess I shouldn't tell you about my cleaning routine spreadsheet, then?" Laughter rumbled in his chest at her widened eyes. "I'm kidding, I'm kidding."

"I get the impression you're one of those people who's totally in control at all times." She watched as he added green peppers to the frying pan and stirred them with a wooden spoon.

"No one is in control of life at all times." He thought for a second. "But I do try to keep a firm hand on things."

I wouldn't mind if he kept a firm hand on me.

Wren stifled a smile as she watched Rhys work the kitchen like a pro. He had his back to her, granting her a secret moment to openly admire his ass. The man wore a pair of jeans like nobody's business.

Why had she come here? To torture herself, apparently.

A deep ache built within her. It had been so long since she'd had sex, and with the stress of her fleeing her hometown and getting herself installed at Ainslie Ave, she hadn't made much time for self-appreciation, either. Her hands twitched with the desire to knead the firm muscles beneath his jeans. She could almost imagine how it would feel to clutch that ass as he plunged deep inside her.

"Wren?"

"Huh?" Her cheeks were as hot as an open flame.

"I asked if you're allergic to anything? I should have checked before I decided what to cook."

"Oh no, I'm healthy as an ox." Physically, anyway. Emotionally...not so much. "I'll eat pretty much anything. When you're raised in a tiny town, you don't always get a lot of choice."

"I'm sure small-town living has its perks." Rhys cracked a few eggs into a bowl and whisked them with a fork. "Not that I would ever consider leaving the city."

"Why's that?"

"I like being able to keep busy."

"And *I* like the anonymity of the city." She watched his deft hands making their dinner as gracefully as if he were conducting a symphony. You could tell a lot by watching people use their hands—and it was clear he knew *exactly* how to use his. "It's so freeing to be able to leave the house without people gossiping about your every move."

"That happen a lot to you at home?"

"Oh yeah. It's kind of like being famous without any of the perks."

"Sounds awful."

"It truly is." She sighed. "The worst thing is that people don't hesitate to make things up."

"Why let the truth get in the way of a good story, right?" He shook his head. "I really don't get why people thrive on gossip. There's so many more interesting things out there in the world."

"Couldn't agree more."

Within minutes Rhys had put two perfectly formed vegetable omelets onto pristine white plates. The scent of garlic, cheese and eggs made Wren's mouth water. She realized then that she'd barely eaten all day. Too busy worrying about the fate of her internship…and the possibility of what might happen if she saw Rhys again.

Time to find out.

"So, do you have any idea who might be behind the security issues at the gallery?" They took their seats at a small table with two chairs. The space was cozy and her knees brushed against his.

"Not yet. Today was just a preliminary meeting. Quinn will be running the investigation, so she'll most likely be back to ask more questions and help Sean set up a proper security system."

"A proper security system?" The omelet seemed to stick in her throat. There went her hopes of trying to break into the storage room again.

She'd found out during her first week that he didn't have any security cameras when she'd asked if there was a backup procedure for the camera tapes. She'd dodged suspicion with a false story about her duties at the community center back home, and he'd told her that he didn't believe in keeping an eye on his staff in that way.

"Yeah, I can't believe he doesn't have a proper security monitoring system in place already. If his paintings are worth that much, it seems crazy not to have cameras."

Wren chewed slowly. She was positive Sean had the money for security cameras. Which meant he chose not to have them because he didn't want footage of the inside of his gallery. All the more reason to suspect he was doing something illegal or, at the very least, unethical.

"Well, it doesn't matter anyway," Rhys said. "We'll find whoever did this. And if they've committed a crime, we'll hand them over to the police."

Had she committed a crime? Did going through someone's emails count as an offense?

All the more reason for her not to say anything to Rhys. She couldn't risk getting fired and possibly fined—or, God forbid, arrested—just for the sake of a romantic fling.

"That does seem crazy. Well, I hope you find whoever is doing these things." Guilt twinged in her gut, but she reminded herself why she was here—to help her friend. The usually confident and bubbly Kylie had come home a shell of her former self, and she deserved payback. "This omelet is incredible, by the way. Thanks for cooking."

He reached for the bottle of wine and topped up her glass. "I'm just being neighborly and returning the favor."

"You patched me up when I cut myself—that debt was already paid."

"Maybe I just wanted to see you again."

The sound of their silverware clicking and scraping filled Wren's pause. "I'm surprised, given what happened. I shouldn't have kicked you out like that. It was rude."

"That night *has* been on my mind." He sipped his wine and Wren watched him, transfixed, as the muscles in his throat worked as he swallowed. Everything about him was so strong, so sure. So powerful and yet controlled. Restrained. "I've thought about it a lot."

"You've thought about that night or just my painting?"

"All of it. I wasn't lying when I said I was going to make a move, Wren."

The confident way he spoke told her he wasn't used to being rejected. And who would say no to him? Not only was he hotter than Hades, but the man was an utter gentleman. A rare combination in her experience.

"You can tell me to stop being pushy," he added with a sly grin. "It's a bad habit, I know. I can be single-minded like that."

Grateful for the opportunity to delay addressing her attraction to him, she reached for her wine. "You're driven. That's not a bad thing."

"*Driven* sounds much better. Mom jokes I was born with a life plan in my hand."

"I bet she's very proud of you."

RHYS TRIED NOT to grimace at Wren's kind—and no doubt well-intended—words. If only it were true. His mother *was* proud of him; she just happened to prefer expressing that pride from a distance.

"My family is complicated," he said eventually.

"Aren't all families?" She shot him an empathetic look. "I don't think 'unconditional love' is as cut-and-dried as people would like to believe."

"Or as equally handed out."

"I'm the sister of an aspiring doctor. I get it." Her head bobbed slowly. "Who's the golden child, brother or sister?"

"Stepbrother."

"Ouch."

"I can't hate the guy. We've been best friends since we were in elementary school. It was like one of those kids' movies. His parents were divorced and my mother was a widow." Part of him felt disloyal for spilling his family drama to Wren. He loved his family. But in the short space of time he'd known Wren he'd become comfortable around her. He trusted her. "When my mom married his dad I thought it was the best thing that could have happened. But it got difficult as the years went on."

She tucked her feet up under her and cradled the wineglass in both hands. Her cascading golden hair and long, flowing skirt made her look like a goddess who'd stepped off a canvas.

"Why did things change?"

"We got older. I started to understand the way the world worked." He kneaded at the knots in the back of his neck. "You see, my dad was black but my mom's white. And my stepfather and stepbrother are white, as well. Which meant I spent a lot of time being asked if I was adopted."

"That would be awful," she said quietly.

"Yeah, it's tough enough being mixed. You feel like you don't truly belong in either camp. And I wasn't really bullied at school, but I was always on the fringe of things. Nothing I did ever got me into the inner circle of any group." He rubbed his palms against his thighs. "What made it worse was that my mom only saw my dad when she looked at me. So after a while it seemed as if she stopped looking."

He'd never said that aloud to anyone before, never admitted that his mother had all but ignored his presence for a portion of his life. And the older he got, the worse it had become.

When he looked back at old photos of his dad, he could see why. Despite the difference in the depth of their skin color, he had his father's full lips and strong jaw. He had the same intense eyes and heavy brows. The same strong cheekbones and slightly too-big ears. Ears made for listening, his mother had called them once.

It dawned on him then that this was why Wren's painting had made such an impact on him. It wasn't just that she'd been thinking about him, it was that she'd been *looking* at him. Acknowledging him.

In her head he was real and present and alive.

"I ended up moving to the city so I didn't have to

keep haunting her like that," he said, shutting out his revelation.

"You moved because you were haunting someone and I moved because I was *being* haunted. Can't win, can we?" she asked with a shake of her head.

"The reason you're haunted, does it have something to do with the painting I saw?" He cleared his throat. "The one of the naked woman."

"My problem was about the paintings," she said with an emphasis on the *s*. "I have a series of them. And, yeah, that's part of the reason I left. My town wasn't quite ready for something so 'shocking' as the naked body."

"I guess some of those towns can be quite conservative."

"Oh, I knew that. It's the whole reason I never showed the paintings to anyone except a few people I trusted in the art community. But my ex found them and…he got pretty mad."

"Why the hell would he be mad about a couple of paintings?"

"He thought I was going to cause a scandal." She laughed, but the sound was hollow. Humorless. "He had grand plans to be a district attorney one day and eventually make a move into politics. He told me he couldn't be with someone who was going to ruin his career with sinful, disgusting activities."

Rhys's chest clenched. The pain in her voice was palpable. "Your ex is an idiot."

"It wouldn't have been so bad if he'd just dumped me and moved on. But oh no, Christian thought *he'd* been wronged, and he wanted to take me down a couple of pegs. Teach me a lesson." Her jaw tightened. "He took photos of the paintings and showed them to people in town to make sure there was no chance any of my 'filthy secrets' could come back to bite him. I could never be the kind of woman he wanted by his side, but he also didn't want anyone else to have me…so he made sure I was 'damaged goods' as far as the town was concerned."

Rhys blinked. "Are you serious?"

"I wish I wasn't. But that tells you a lot about our relationship," she snorted.

"And people really thought a few nude paintings were that bad?"

"I didn't really have the chance to tell my side of the story. Christian went to a few loud voices in the community and the rumors were all over town before I had the chance to do anything about it. He said he felt it was his 'duty' to make sure I wasn't working with any children while I was creating pornographic material."

"I don't even know what to say." Rhys shook his head, trying to quash the anger that had bubbled up in him. "That's ridiculous."

"Anyway, enough of my sob story." A smile tugged at her lips. "It's all in the past, and I'm here now."

But for how long? The question hung at the edge of his mind.

Why can't you stop planning the future for once and live in the now? Live in the now with her.

"I'm glad you're here," he said.

Her dazzling smile kindled warmth in his chest. "And I'm glad you didn't let me bleed out in the hallway."

"My first-aid skills are good, but I've got other skills that are better than that."

"You're a fabulous cook, too."

Hunger gnawed at him. "That's not what I meant."

Her pupils dilated, the black centers eating away at

the rim of blue around them. Her chest rose and fell rapidly, causing her breasts to press against the thin tank top and reveal the faint shadow of her nipples. Her hand fluttered at her collarbone, toying with a thin necklace.

She intoxicated him. The very sight of her was so addictive that he was already desperate for a taste, as though he knew just how delicious she would be.

"I'll do the dishes," she said, standing and reaching for his plate. As she leaned over he could see that her blush extended down her neck and across her chest, coloring her skin with a rosy hue. "It's only fair since you cooked."

She stacked the plates in her arms and headed off in the direction of his kitchen. Draining the rest of the wine in his glass, he gave her a moment. Wren was skittish and now he understood the reason for that. She'd been hurt— run out of her hometown by a vindictive, selfish bastard.

But he *also* knew when a woman was attracted to him—and Wren's face hid nothing.

Collecting the glasses and the half-empty bottle of wine, he followed her. In the small space, he could feel the heat radiating around them. Neither had said a word, but the air held a sizzling tension. Anticipation raced through his veins.

"Please, stop helping," she said as she collected the dirty saucepan and wooden spoon from the stove. "Let me do it."

She brushed past him, her bare arm sweeping against his. The subtle touch sent shock waves through him, flipping the on switch to his entire nervous system. It caught the on switch to his cock as well, which stood to full attention, straining against the fly of his jeans.

Holy hell. He couldn't seem to control himself around

her. Turning as though he were about to rinse the wine-glasses in the sink, he adjusted himself.

"It's no trouble." He flipped the taps on, but the water gushed out far stronger than he'd expected and it sprayed him all down his front.

"Oh no!" She clamped a hand over her mouth. "The taps here have a mind of their own. I swear they're haunted by evil water ghosts."

She reached for the dish towel and wadded it up in her hand, pressing it straight to the wet patch on his stomach, dabbing up and down.

If he'd thought he was hard before, he was like marble now.

Her hand drifted over him, hovering at his waist as her eyes caught on the totally noticeable bulge in his jeans. Cheeks flaming, she sucked on her bottom lip and drew her hand back as if burned. Shit, she probably thought he was some sex-crazed freak.

"Wren, I'm sor—"

"You'll need to lose it." Her eyes came up to meet his like two smoldering sapphires.

"Huh?"

"The T-shirt." She flicked her hand in his direction. "A dish towel won't fix that. It has to come off."

He hesitated for a moment but the lust in her eyes urged him on. Curling his fingers under the hem of the now-soaked cotton shirt, he peeled it up and over his head. Cool air swept over his skin, tightening his nipples and making him hyperaware of every inch of his body.

"The jeans, too," she said, keeping his face straight. "They're soaked."

He glanced down and saw a small dark patch where

the denim had absorbed the water. They were hardly soaked. "You sure about that?"

"Let me help you." She stepped forward and reached for the buckle on his belt.

Her fingertips grazed his bare skin and he had to stifle a moan. He might have started the fire, but she was fanning the flames.

6

WASN'T SHE SUPPOSED to be keeping her distance? At the very least she should be drawing boundaries, given he was the guy who could get her in a world of trouble right now.

Then why did you come here? You knew where this would go. He won't leave your head until you do something about it.

Her fingers trembled as they wrapped around the sturdy leather of his belt, grazing the hard ridge pressing against his fly. His hips jerked as she released the buckle.

"Christ, Wren." He uttered her name so low she almost didn't hear it. But he only took a second before he grabbed her hips and pinned her against the kitchen counter. "I thought I was going to be the one to make a move."

"So move," she said, taunting him softly.

A gasp escaped her lips as he nudged his leg between hers, his thigh applying just the right amount of pressure to the needy ache there.

"Yes." The word slipped from her lips and Wren felt

her last remaining ounce of restraint disappear into the ether.

What did Debbie say—you've got to use it before you lose it?

Maybe it was stupid to get entangled with Rhys. No, it was *definitely* stupid. And not only that, it was irresponsible and selfish. She was keeping secrets from this man who'd been nothing but kind to her. Even after she'd spilled out all the pain of what had happened to her back home.

Stupid, stupid, stupid.

But right now her brain wasn't the one in the driver's seat. So there would be no obeying the speed limit, no following the rules. Her body had taken over, and it wanted to make up for lost time.

"How do you feel about dessert?" she asked.

Hard granite dug into her lower back as his hips held her fast. "What do you have in mind?"

"Let's skip whatever you had planned and go straight to bed."

"Health conscious. I like it." His hot breath whispered across her skin as his full lips grazed her cheek.

"Yes, *exactly* what I was going for." She rolled her eyes, her laugh breaking off into a moan as he nipped at her earlobe. "Do you have to be such an adult about everything?"

"I'm thinking some very adult things right now."

Her hands drifted up his chest, tracing each ridge of muscle one by one. "Oh yeah?"

"Super adult. It would make my spreadsheet look like child's play."

Laughter bubbled up in Wren's chest as she placed a finger over his lips. "Okay, enough dirty talk."

Mercifully, he brushed her hand aside and finally captured her mouth. The soft glide of his tongue against hers left her weak at the knees. He tasted of wine and heaven. Boy, oh boy, could he kiss.

This was A-grade, five-gold-stars, Nobel Prize levels of kissing.

His hands were at her waist, then her rib cage, then her breasts. Kneading. Squeezing. Flicking.

"Oh!" Her head jerked back as he pinched her nipple through the thin layer of her tank. It felt as though a volt of electricity had shot straight through her.

"Is that a good 'oh'?" He chuckled against the side of her neck as he nipped at the sensitive skin there. Each bite was soothed with a swipe of his tongue in a maddening pattern. Nip. Swipe. Nip. Swipe.

"That's a 'don't stop if you know what's good for you' oh," she said, lolling her head back as his fingers hooked under the strap of her tank and pulled it down, exposing her breast to his hands.

His palm circled her, only stopping to allow his thumb to take over. And then his mouth… Oh, dear God. His mouth. He drew her nipple between his teeth, holding it gently there while he flicked his tongue against her, drawing out every soul-deep pleasure sound she could possible make.

Shamelessly, she rubbed against him. It had been so long since she'd felt this good, strung tighter than a wire and ready to snap. His other hand fisted in her skirt, trying to get at her through all the layers of fabric.

"Dammit," he growled against her breast. "This skirt is ridiculous."

"It's not ridiculous."

"It is." He stood back and watched, his dark eyes almost totally black as they drank her in. "No, it's criminal. Hiding those legs away should be illegal."

Laughing, she made a show of swinging her hips like an exotic dancer. "Well, I do *not* want to get arrested."

"Ditch the skirt."

A sharp sound pierced the air as she drew the zipper down, and in an instant the fabric puddled at her feet. The heel of his palm found her center, grinding a series of slow, intense circles against her sex. Her clit ached, desperate for friction and release.

"Yes," she gasped, running her hands around the back of his head as he suckled her breast. His hair was so short there was nothing for her to grab on to, but that didn't stop her from trying.

His mouth came back up to hers as his hand shifted, a finger breaching the edge of her panties to softly stroke the seam of her sex. He'd be able to feel just how wet she was, how insanely aroused and excited. But she didn't care—couldn't care. Not while he was pushing her so close to an orgasm she knew would shatter her completely.

"Rhys…uh!" The words dissolved on her tongue as he kissed her, the tip of his finger pressing against her entrance.

"Are you ready?" His words were rough, sharp. Like gravel. "Are you ready to feel my fingers inside you?"

"Please, please." She couldn't string any more words together, so she looped her arms around his neck and pressed her lips to his ear. "Yes."

The second he slid a finger inside her she thought she'd break. Her internal muscles clenched around him immediately, trying to draw him all the way in. But he held on to his control, sliding in and out slowly. Easing her into it. Stretching her.

She ground her hips against his hand and moaned, cursing under her breath. Then he shifted, curling his finger at just the right angle, rubbing the little bundle of nerves deep inside her and that was it. Game over.

"Oh. My. God." Her body shook and she tumbled, wave after wave of pleasure crashing over her. Filling her. Drowning her.

He held her there until it subsided. Until her heart slowed and her breath came in longer beats. Until she was able to stand on her own. Only then did he withdraw his hand and kiss her trembling lips.

"See. So much better than spreadsheets," she said with a shaky laugh.

"Couldn't agree more." A chuckle rumbled deep in his chest and he bundled her up in his arms, the hard length of his arousal pressing into her belly.

Almost immediately her hunger returned. At full force.

Her fingertips grazed him, feeling the strength of him through the cotton of his boxer briefs. She wasn't done yet, not by a long shot. Finding the slit in his underwear, she snaked her hand in and wrapped her fingers around him. He was hot against her palm, thick and heavy. *Very* thick.

She swallowed. She hadn't been with many men during her somewhat lackluster sex life. And *none* of them had felt like Rhys. The sheer virility of him thrilled her. Smoothing her hand up and down, she squeezed tentatively and was rewarded with a low, ragged groan.

Then she remembered. *Condoms.*

They hadn't exactly been high up on her shopping list

when she'd fled to New York, so she hoped he would be better prepared. She didn't want to stop now; she didn't know if she had the strength to walk away without experiencing that long, hard length inside her.

"Shall we move this party to the bedroom?" he said as his lips brushed the shell of her ear.

"I'm hoping you're prepared."

"If you're talking about protection, of course. I didn't want to be presumptuous but…" He grinned.

"You *are* a Boy Scout. I knew it."

He grabbed her hand and led her toward his bedroom. "Come on. If I don't have you now I'm going to burst."

"Is that a fact?"

She couldn't deny how good his attraction made her feel. It smoothed over her, filling in the cracks and dents and chips in her confidence. It restored her. Made her believe that she was a sexy, young woman who could start over. Start fresh.

"One hundred percent." He drew her to him by the waist, his large hands skating around to her lower back and pressing her against him.

"Not a hundred and ten?" she teased.

"There is no more than a hundred percent."

Her calves hit the edge of his bed as he backed her up. Drawing his eyes away only for a moment, he yanked open the top drawer of his bedside table and rummaged around until he produced a foil packet. Then he tossed it onto the bed and returned to her.

"Now we're prepared," she said, her palms running up and down her thighs. Unsure where to start.

"More." The word came out so strangled, so forced that it fueled her on.

She slipped her hands between her legs to brush against her drenched panties. "Like this?"

"Hell. Yes."

She whipped the tank over her head and turned, tipping forward from her waist so that her hands landed on the bed and her ass waved high in the air. A guttural groan came from behind her, and a moment later he was pressed against her. Rough hands held her in place as he rubbed the hard length of his cock against her ass.

"Holy shit, Wren. You're incredible." His fingers hooked into the waistband of her panties and pulled them over her ass and down her legs. "Stay there and let me look."

Her whole body clenched as cool air drifted across her sex. She'd never done anything like this before. Sex with her previous boyfriends had been bland as cardboard. But she hadn't known anything else. This, however, seemed natural. Clearly, she'd been missing out.

Then she felt his cock press against her inner thigh, smudging moisture against her. A second later the sound of foil tearing broke through their heavy breathing, and Wren turned to face him, watching him roll the condom down his length.

"We'll go slow, okay?" His palm cupped her face and she kissed his hand.

"Yes, please." She reached out to touch him, her fingers skating over the swollen head of his cock.

He eased her back against the bed and used his strong thighs to part her softer ones. The contrast of his warm, brown skin against her fairness sucked the breath out of her lungs. He was so beautiful. So confident and capable and strong.

Yet there was a gentleness to him, a level of care that she wasn't used to.

Closing her eyes, she breathed in the surroundings. The scent of sex, the unique male aroma mingling with clean laundry, a hint of cologne. She wanted to absorb it all.

"You still with me, Wren?" His lips brushed over her jaw and down her neck.

"All the way." Her fingers raked down his back as he shifted forward, the head of his cock pressing against her opening.

"Tell me how it feels, okay?" His hand cupped her breast, and he rolled a nipple between his thumb and forefinger.

"Amazing." The word dissolved into a cry as he pushed inside her, filling her. Taking her.

She sucked in a breath and let it out slowly, willing her body to relax into it. As he started moving, all the blood in her body rushed south and she melted against him. Each stroke pushed her higher and higher, his hips bumping her as he built up speed.

He rained kisses down over her. "You feel so good wrapped around me like that."

"Wrapped around you?" A wicked smile curved on her mouth and she lifted her hips, anchoring her legs around his waist. Urging him to go deeper. Drawing him in.

"Wren!" His hips jerked and he pumped into her, the rhythm frantic as they chased pleasure.

The muscles in his arms corded as he thrust, and she gripped him, digging her nails into his skin. Marking him as hers. Her name fell from his lips as he shuddered inside her.

The silence washed over her as they lay there, tangled

in one another, and a deep calm claimed her. Maybe her sister had been right all along. Sex was just what she needed to feel in charge of her life again.

RHYS HOVERED IN that fuzzy stage between sleep and wakefulness as sunlight breached the gaps in his blinds.

Last night had been everything he'd wanted. He and Wren had shared a physical connection that could only be described as electric. Together, their bodies just... worked.

After a steamy shower together, they'd tumbled back into bed and slept soundly until he'd reached for her in the middle of the night. In the darkness everything was new; he'd learned her body all over again. Mapped it with his hands and his tongue. Explored every inch of her until sleep had claimed them once more.

His muscles ached as he stretched, his hand gravitating toward her as if that instinct had already been ground into his subconscious. But his palm connected with a flat surface. Blinking, he pushed up to a sitting position and surveyed the room.

No Wren.

"You have to wake up to reality at some point," he said to himself.

They hadn't exactly made any promises to one another last night—it had been raw and unbridled. Spontaneous. Without expectation.

In other words, the total opposite to how he did everything in his life.

He rolled out of bed and padded into the kitchen. The rush of early morning traffic greeted him from the open window, highlighting the quietness of his apartment. Still no Wren. Disappointment curled low in his gut.

He'd been hoping to wake up with her and perhaps extend their night of passion into the morning. Before he had the chance to decide how to handle her stealthy exit, his work ringtone cut through the silence and he grabbed the phone from the coffee table.

"Rhys?" Quinn's excited voice made him cringe. "I'm glad you're already up."

He looked at the screen. It wasn't even seven thirty, and Quinn was notoriously *not* a morning person. "How much coffee have you had?"

"Not much," she said in a way that told him she was well and truly caffeinated. "When do you think you'll be in?"

His gaze swept over the empty apartment. It wasn't as if he had anything to hang around for given that Wren had vanished. "I'll be leaving in a few minutes. Why?"

"I couldn't sleep last night, so I was doing some digging on Sean Ainslie and his employees. I found some interesting stuff."

If this were any other job he would have told Quinn to run with the information and only come to him when she got stuck—managing the tech side of security for Cobalt & Dane kept him too busy to be involved in every single assignment. But he wanted to keep an eye on the situation in case things became dangerous. It wasn't too long ago that a seemingly ordinary information security job had resulted in Quinn being cornered alone by a person connected to their client.

He didn't want anything to happen that might put Quinn—or Wren—in the crosshairs.

"Keep digging," he said, heading back into his bedroom. "I'll find you when I get in and you can bring me up to speed."

By the time Rhys made it into the office, Quinn was almost bouncing off the walls. She sat at one of the senior security consultant's desks and was talking a hundred miles a minute.

"You'll have to cut her off, Rhys," Owen said, laughter crinkling his eyes. "If she consumes any more sugar and caffeine she'll launch into outer space."

"I haven't had *that* much," Quinn protested, her smile bright and slightly too wide.

"Her eyeballs are vibrating."

Rhys shook his head. "You have to take better care of yourself. Coffee is no substitute for sleep."

Owen snorted. "Have you seen what she drinks? You can't call that coffee. It's basically a liquefied energy bar."

"Come on." Rhys tilted his head toward the boardroom. "Let's go through what you found."

"I invited Owen to sit in," Quinn said as the three of them headed to the empty room. "He's got capacity at the moment, so he can accompany me on the site visits rather than taking up more of your time."

They all took a seat at the large boardroom-style table. The room was often set up as a "war room" for big assignments and strategy planning.

"Are you sure you've got capacity, Owen?" Rhys leaned back in his chair and kept his tone even. "I don't want to take you away from any other assignments that Logan has you working on."

The senior consultants all reported straight up to Logan Dane, so there was no way Rhys could tell Owen *not* to assist Quinn with the case, especially if he'd been directed to lend a hand by the big boss.

But that didn't mean he would let go of the assignment completely, either. Not while Wren could be at risk.

"I'm more than happy to help out," Owen replied with an easygoing shrug. "Quinn told me there are some tech security elements, which is out of my realm, but I understand there could be some physical security elements, as well. She mentioned a possible break-in attempt."

The technology and information security stuff fell squarely in Rhys's territory thanks to the years he'd spent helping banks protect their information. But Owen was a former police officer and had come from a background that made security a key component of his life. A personal obsession, one might say. Between Quinn and Rhys's tech smarts and Owen's robust experience, they made the perfect team.

Whatever was going on at Ainslie Ave, they would figure it out quickly and quietly.

"There was a failed attempt to access a locked storage room, but the owner of the gallery couldn't find any signs of a break-in to the gallery itself," Rhys said.

Owen nodded. "So we're looking at the possibility of an inside job."

"It *is* possible." Quinn flipped open her laptop. "But the gallery owner himself is behaving strangely. He's got this expensive security system for the one storage room and an alarm system for the building. Yet he has *no* security cameras inside the gallery. It's possible someone who's not a staff member got inside without setting off any alarms, but we have zero proof because there's no footage."

"So what did you find last night?" Rhys asked, eager to move the conversation along. He drummed his fingers against the top of the desk.

"I was digging around to see if the client has had a falling-out with anyone, or has any shady connections that might point to who's behind the break-in attempt. Sean Ainslie comes from a very wealthy family. Old money. His father was also a judge, and he retired a few years ago, so I wondered if he might have enemies."

"Okay," Rhys said. "And?"

"That's not what I found." She held up her hand when he huffed with impatience. "The website has profiles for all the interns that he currently has working for them: Lola, Wren and Aimee."

"So what?"

"Well, the old profiles of the past employees are still saved in the back end of the gallery's website. I compiled all the head shots." Quinn turned her laptop around so Owen and Rhys could see the screen. "Do you detect a common theme?"

Fifteen young female faces stared back at him. Wren's fair skin and blue eyes immediately captured his attention. In the photo, she was laughing. Her eyes shone like they had last night when he'd taken her to bed.

Memories flooded him, his body instantly recalling the feeling of her hands on his chest. Cupping his face. His ass as he thrust into her.

"Boss?" Quinn waved a hand in front of him. "I said, 'Do you detect a common theme?'"

"They're all young women." He shrugged. "What's your point?"

"*Attractive* young women," Owen added. "Are you thinking that he might have become involved with his interns?"

Quinn nodded. "It's very possible. Especially since

I found photos of him with a few of these women at industry events."

Rhys's stomach churned at the thought of Sean hitting on Wren. "Go on."

"One news article references a huge fight he had with a Marguerite Bernard. It said that his gallery was hosting a show for another local artist but the night ended abruptly when the couple had a huge screaming match and he kicked everyone out. According to her website she started working at a different gallery a few months later."

"It could just be a lover's quarrel," Rhys said.

"I wouldn't have thought much of it until I saw this." She reached around the computer and brought up another picture.

It was a picture of a woman. Swelling had almost closed her eye over completely and an eggplant-colored bruise mottled her fair complexion. The skin appeared to be split across her cheekbone.

"Shit," Owen muttered, shaking his head in disgust.

Rhys grunted in agreement and clenched his fists.

"This is Marguerite Bernard," Quinn continued. "This picture was posted on her Instagram page two days after the incident at the gallery. The caption says, 'He will get away with this. His father will protect him and I won't have the chance for justice. Remember, control is not love.' There are a bunch of hashtags under it, as well. She doesn't reference Sean by name, but the timing certainly fits."

Fighting back the sick feeling in his stomach, Rhys tried to focus on the job at hand. Now, with even more reason to be worried for Wren's safety, he needed to ensure that they handled this situation accordingly. Knowing Quinn's background and recent experience, she might want to jump in and blame Ainslie. But they had to tread carefully, refrain from doing anything that might spook him until they had more information.

Which meant Rhys needed to play devil's advocate.

"I understand this is very disturbing," he said. "But I still don't see what this has to do with the potential break-ins. Do you think Marguerite might have done it?"

"Not necessarily, but I've looked into a few of the other women who've worked for Ainslie, and a number didn't stay at the gallery very long." She closed the lid on her laptop. "I'm going to reach out to them and ask if they experienced anything shady about Ainslie's practices."

"You seem to be treating him like a suspect rather than a client," Rhys warned.

Her head bobbed. "I have a funny feeling about this guy. Something doesn't seem right, but point taken. I'll be discreet."

"I thought Quinn and I might head over to the gallery later today so I can suss this guy out," Owen added. "Can't hurt to get another set of eyes on him, right?"

"Of course." Rhys nodded. "I want to be kept fully updated on this assignment. Okay, Quinn?"

"Are you worried that I won't be able to handle it?" Her eyes narrowed at him.

He drew a deep breath. Quinn's insecurities had certainly improved since she'd started dating Aiden, but her journey to confidence wasn't one that would happen overnight. Just as her defensive shield still popped up from time to time.

"Did I say that?"

"No," she admitted.

"I've met with the client. Therefore, my name is stamped on this, and I don't take that lightly." He turned to Owen. "Quinn will run with this assignment and you can provide guidance and mentoring as appropriate."

Owen nodded. "Got it."

Rhys stood. "Good. I expect an update tomorrow morning."

In the meantime, he would have to stay occupied so he didn't drive himself crazy over Wren. No easy task, since her beautiful face appeared the second his brain wasn't fully engaged on a task.

It's just a fling. She's already made it clear that she's not going to stay, and the sooner you believe that, the saner you'll be.

Unfortunately for Rhys, knowing she was leaving didn't necessarily mean he could avoid wanting her to stay.

7

THE LAST FEW days had been a whirlwind for Wren. She'd felt guilty ever since leaving Rhys's apartment at the crack of dawn on Tuesday morning. Now it was Friday and she hadn't seen him all week. Maybe she should have stayed. Morning-after etiquette wasn't exactly her forte, and she'd wanted to save him the trouble of having to kick her out. Or, rather, saving herself the humiliation of *being* kicked out.

Watching his beautiful sleeping form had stirred some uneasy emotions inside her. She was supposed to be in New York to figure out what'd happened to her friend. *Not* to be picking up devastatingly attractive men and using them to broaden her sexual horizons.

But Rhys wasn't just that. The way he'd made her feel…hell, it was soul-soothing. Healing. It was about the sex and yet it wasn't.

Which made her guilt over lying to him so much stronger. Not to mention that she'd yet to make any progress at the gallery.

"You'll bury yourself with all those thoughts," she muttered to herself as she lugged her canvas up the last flight of stairs to her apartment. The messy interpretation of Rhys's face stared at her as she trudged.

At least the dust storm of feelings had the benefit of spurring her into action. She'd decided to take cupcakes to Aimee in the hopes a little "girl time" would butter the woman up and Wren could ask about her relationship with Sean. Turned out buttercream frosting was as good as truth serum.

Aimee must have been looking for a sounding board, because she'd let the information fly as soon as they were alone in the gallery's kitchenette. She'd fought with Sean recently; he'd gotten a little rough. The bruise on Aimee's upper arm was hidden by a floaty top, but there was no denying the distinct finger-shaped marks.

Had Kylie fallen prey to Sean's charms, as well? Wren would never have thought her friend would be the type to get involved with her boss. But there were similarities that Wren couldn't ignore and she already suspected Sean was to blame for Kylie's black eye and fractured bones.

Wren wondered if the email Aimee had tried to delete contained proof of Sean's abuse. Or of their relationship? But when she'd had tried to get back into Sean's email to see what else she could dig up, it looked as though he'd changed the password. After a few failed attempts to get in, she'd reluctantly stopped, afraid that if the password had to be reset he would get suspicious again.

It was yet another day where she'd gone home empty-handed.

From the depths of her bag her phone started to ring. "Dammit," Wren cursed under her breath.

She paused at the top of the staircase, leaning the canvas against the wall while she dug her phone out. "Hello?"

"Big sis!"

"Why do you always seem to call when I'm carrying stuff up stairs?" Wren tucked the phone between her ear and her shoulder. "That's some talent you've got."

"I aim to annoy," Debbie said cheerfully. "How's things? Banged your neighbor yet?"

A strangled noise halfway between laughing and choking came out of Wren's mouth. "What?"

"I take that as a confirmation. Go, you." Her sister laughed. "I hope my pep talk helped things along."

Wren rolled her eyes as she shuffled awkwardly down the corridor with the canvas and her bag. "My sex life has nothing to do with you and that's how it should be."

"Whatever works. Was it amazing? Was *he* amazing?"

"It was and he was, if you must know. Not that it's any of your business." She unlocked her front door and carried the canvas to her empty easel. Staring into her version of Rhys's big warm eyes sent a flutter through her stomach.

"I'm happy for you. Now we don't have to worry about the prune—"

"If you finish that sentence I'm going to come home and throttle you," Wren threatened. "And don't start again with the 'I'm a doctor' BS."

"You're so mean."

"No, I'm setting boundaries. It's a healthy thing to do. You should try it sometime."

Debbie huffed. "Well, I guess I won't bother telling you the real reason I called, then."

Her sister could be a little melodramatic sometimes. Crocodile tears had been her best weapon as a child, her ability to wrap their parents around her little finger far surpassing Wren's natural openness. Part of her used to resent Debbie's way of doing things, but now Wren saw honesty as something to be wary of. Something to be used wisely. Like a currency.

"Spill," she demanded, wandering into the kitchen and flicking on her coffee machine.

"I checked in on Kylie today." Suddenly Debbie's tone was heavier, burdened with emotion.

"How is she?"

"Not good. She's lost a lot of weight." And that was saying something since Kylie was already on the thin side. "She said that someone called her today asking about her work at the gallery."

"Did she say who it was?" Could it have been Rhys? It surely wouldn't take him too long to connect Kylie to Wren. Their hometown was small enough that it would be easy to assume they were acquaintances, at the very least. Perhaps Sean had said something.

"Some girl. Kylie was so flustered by the call that she didn't think to get her name." Debbie sighed.

It must have been Quinn. "Right."

"She was seriously shaken up. They were asking about whether or not she had a relationship with the gallery owner."

"Why would they want to know that?"

"I have no idea."

Wren rubbed her hand over her face. "Did Kylie catch where they were calling from? Was it the police?"

"No. A security company, I think she said."

Definitely Quinn.

Debbie paused. "Tell me you're safe, Birdie."

The concern in her sister's voice made a crushing weight land on Wren's chest. "I'm fine, I promise."

"Kylie was asking about you again. I told her you

were probably being brainwashed on your 'art retreat' into some tree-hugging, plant-eating hippie as we speak."

She could practically hear her sister rolling her eyes. "Good."

"In all seriousness, though, you should come home soon. I'm doing my best, but she's closer to you and I don't think she's telling me everything about what happened."

"I'll email her. But I don't have any results yet, so I can't come home."

"What exactly do you think you're going to find? This seems like a wild freaking goose chase."

Wren swallowed and reached for a mug from the rack next to the sink. The floral design had a chunk taken out of it from when she'd accidentally knocked it over while cooking dinner one night. Her fingertip traced the imperfection.

"I don't know," she admitted. "But there's something up with this Ainslie guy. I can just…feel it. He's doing something bad, and I'd bet my last ten dollars that what happened to Kylie wasn't a first."

"Please be careful."

"I'm *fine*, Debs. Cross my heart." She poured her coffee and hoped that the false confidence in her voice was enough to placate her sister.

"Okay. I'll leave you alone, but I'm calling again in a few days and I don't want you to give me this 'I need boundaries' bullshit. I'm your sister and I will find you so I can whip your ass, if necessary."

"You're getting all Liam Neeson on me," Wren teased. "Are you going to threaten me with your 'very particular set of skills'?"

"Damn straight I am. Now swear to me you'll check in more often?"

"I solemnly swear to check in more often." She smiled in spite of herself. "Hand on heart."

They finished the call a moment later after Debs gave her another "pep talk" about her sex life. The woman couldn't seem to go one phone call without bringing it up. She was twenty-three, though. So perhaps being at college meant she had sex on the brain.

"*You* have sex on the brain," she said to herself with a shake of her head.

The last few days had been a giant waste of time. Instead of being able to concentrate on her work, her head had been full of Rhys. Not just because the sex had been amazing, but because she'd felt amazing afterward.

With Christian, sex had been like a field of land mines. Sometimes she'd navigated it safely, sometimes not. It was impossible to tell what would set him off—it might be that she suggested something he considered "dirty" or that her body didn't respond the way he'd expected.

He was a product of his uptight, guilt-focused upbringing. His messed-up views on sex—and now, with space from him, she *knew* they were messed up—had caused her a lot of angst. Which often made it hard for her to fully enjoy sex. And that meant she often couldn't relax during the act itself.

But Rhys was different. With him she was free to be herself. For the first time in her life she felt sexy and beautiful. Amazing as the orgasms were, it wasn't the most important part. It was laying in his arms afterward, feeling safe and secure and wanted. Not feeling judged.

A tiny voice in the back of her mind niggled at her. *Why stop at one night?*

She wasn't going to be in New York for too long, so that meant there was no risk of anything long-term. No risk of him getting the idea that he had some claim or control over her.

But there was the slight problem of the fact that he was the one person she *should* keep at a distance. Her desire for him battled with her desire to get revenge for her friend. He was the one person who could put a stop to her helping Kylie. And she wasn't yet sure she could trust him to keep her secret and not hand her over to the police.

Then you'll just have to keep your lips shut and talk with your body. It's about time you took what you wanted without worrying about anyone else—you're done with that!

BY THREE O'CLOCK Rhys was driving himself to distraction. With Quinn out of the office and working on the Ainslie Ave assignment, he felt disconnected from his job. He wanted to know what was going on—but checking in too often would only lead to trouble. Either Quinn would get suspicious, or she would think he doubted her.

Neither of which he wanted.

But knowing that didn't help him focus on work. After rearranging his already-neat drawers, wiping down his desk and alphabetizing his books, he'd had enough. Now he was jogging upstairs to his apartment, craving a run. His nervous energy had to be burned off.

Ever since Monday night his body had been wired. Electrified. Buzzing.

As he bounded up the last few steps, he caught sight of Wren's door. His feet carried him toward it without his brain having a chance to react. This had been his game the last few days, wanting to see her but resisting.

His willpower slowly wearing down until now it was merely a whisper.

Maybe he should check if she was home, just in case.

"Just in case what?" he muttered to himself. "She'll probably be at work, anyway."

At that moment—like some kind of sign from the heavens—music started to play inside her apartment. It floated through the door, tempting him.

You should check in and ask about Ainslie. You know, because of the assignment.

His brain had conveniently pushed aside the fact that Quinn would have already asked those questions. But right now he was clutching at straws for an excuse to see Wren that didn't have anything to do with the fact that she'd left in the middle of the night.

He raised his hand to the door and knocked twice. When she opened it, Rhys wondered if he'd accidentally found a secret gate to heaven. The scent of chocolate wafted out and Wren stood there looking like a vision. She had on a white tank top, her long legs exposed by a pair of tiny denim shorts. Her hair was held back with a red head scarf.

A dark streak marred her cheekbone. "Uh, hi," she said, a flush immediately creeping across her skin.

"You have a little something…" He reached out and swiped at the mark. "Chocolate or paint?"

"Chocolate. I'm baking brownies." Her eyes glimmered. "Would you like to come in?"

"Sure. I had a few questions for you about the gallery, if that's okay?"

"Of course." Was it his imagination or did her eyes dim at the mention of her work? "That shouldn't stop me from serving up some dessert, should it?"

"Hell, no."

She held the door open for him and he stepped inside. The kitchen was a disaster zone; there were mixing bowls and wooden spoons piled up in the sink. A bag of sugar had tipped over and spilled fine crystals onto the countertop. Packets of ingredients littered the bench. As Rhys followed her to the source of the glorious scent, something crunched beneath his shoe.

A walnut.

"Sorry for the state of the kitchen," she said with a nervous laugh. "I'm a messy cook. But I promise the taste will be worth it."

He toyed with the idea of sharing his process for "cleaning as you go" that kept his kitchen near spotless while he cooked. But the words halted in his mouth as Wren bent over to open the oven. His mouth watered, and it wasn't from the intensified scent of chocolate brownies.

The sight of her shapely ass being thrust high in the air as she tipped forward, red oven mitts on her hands, damn near fried his brain cells.

"It's fine," he managed to get out as she straightened up and placed the baked goods onto a wooden cutting block. "I would say 'me, too' but you'd see right through that."

"You're right." She laughed. "I wouldn't believe it for a second. I bet your kitchen is cleaner after you've finished cooking than mine is before I've started."

"I'm going to plead the Fifth on that one," he said.

"You know, getting messy isn't always a bad thing," she said as she dipped the knife into the center.

Gooey melted chocolate clung to the blade. She swiped her fingertip along it, gathering up the excess batter before popping it into her mouth. Watching her lips wrap around her finger sent a bolt of lust through him.

Damn, she could make even the simplest things look tempting as sin.

"You had some questions for me?" she asked, her lip twitching with a cheeky smile.

"I do. Did you end up meeting with Quinn or anyone else from Cobalt & Dane in the last few days?"

She shook her head as she sliced up the brownies. "No, I believe they came in on Tuesday but I only worked half a day. I think Aimee and Lola spoke with them. And then I was supposed to be painting this afternoon but I couldn't seem to focus, so I brought the canvas home with me. You know, change of scenery and all that."

"So you started baking?"

"It's my favorite method of procrastination." Her delicate hands moved deftly and a few seconds later she pushed a plate toward him.

"Are you still working on my portrait?" He forked a generous piece of the dessert into his mouth and moaned at the perfectly rich, sweet taste.

It had been a hell of a long time since he'd eaten anything this decadent—his diet was designed for optimum nutrition, and that didn't allow for a lot of sweet treats other than the occasional glass of wine.

But Wren's baking was as tempting as she was.

"I am. But I'm feeling a little stuck with it," she admitted. "Sean said if I don't get him a complete painting soon he's going to boot me out of the program."

"That's harsh."

"I understand his point—there are plenty of people who would love to have my spot. But sometimes the creativity just won't come." She sighed. "Anyway, you didn't come here to listen to my woes."

"I could sit for you," he said. "So you can paint me."

"You want to be my model?"

"If it would help. I mean, I can sit and ask the questions I need to ask and you can paint." He cleared his throat. "You know, two birds, one stone and all that. It'll be more efficient that way."

God, he sounded like an idiot. What was it about Wren that got him all tangled up? As if she wouldn't see "more efficient" as a thinly veiled ploy for him to hang around longer.

"That might just be what I need." She abandoned her half-eaten brownie. "What's your modeling experience?"

"Zip."

She grabbed a chair and positioned it in front of her canvas. "Really? I'm surprised."

"Why?"

"You'd make a good model, I think. My life-drawing class would have loved you."

"You've done life drawing?" He settled into the chair and tried to get comfortable.

"Yeah. I had to drive to one of the bigger cities near my hometown to take the classes in secret." The click-clack sound of her setting up her brushes filled the pause in their conversation. "That kind of thing is frowned upon where I come from, given the naked body is *so* sinful." She rolled her eyes.

"Personally, I'm a fan of the naked body."

Memories of their night together flickered in his mind, but he tamped them down. He was here to find out what was going on at the gallery and to make sure that Sean Ainslie was keeping his hands to himself.

Yeah, right, keep telling yourself that.

"So, about the gallery," he started.

"Hmm?" Her eyes looked past the canvas, darting over him as if she were analyzing him down to his bones. Breaking his face up into components and committing them to memory.

"Has Sean Ainslie ever hit on you?"

That question seemed to throw her off-kilter. "No, why?"

"Quinn had a hunch that perhaps he was getting involved with his interns."

"Is that such a bad thing?" She frowned as she turned back to the canvas.

"Not necessarily. But we think he may have assaulted one of his interns previously. Some information points to them being an item."

She stilled on the other side of the canvas. Part of her was hidden, but he could see her hand hovering in front of her. Motionless. "Which intern?"

"A woman named Marguerite. Do you know her?"

"No." She adjusted her bandanna. "But he *is* seeing one of the current interns."

Hmm, so Quinn might have been on the money, after all. "Who?"

"Aimee." Her eyes remained on the canvas.

He made a mental note to check in with Quinn and find out whether she'd come up with that same information. "How do you know that?"

When she dragged her gaze up, guilt painted her features. "I don't want to get anyone in trouble."

"You won't. We're just trying to understand what's going on."

"Aimee told me."

He nodded. "Okay."

"I thought this was supposed to be about a security incident." Her light brows crinkled. "I mean, what does one have to do with the other?"

"We're looking for a motive. If he's abused one of his employees in the past, there's a chance she or someone she knows has targeted him for revenge purposes. I get how they might not seem connected, but we have to consider all angles. And Sean couldn't give us any information on who he suspected might be trying to break into the gallery, so we have to start somewhere."

"If he really has abused his staff, would you blame them for acting out against him?"

"No, but my personal feelings on the situation don't matter. Our job is to make sure we find out who's been breaking into the gallery and into Sean's emails." He paused for a moment. "If there's evidence that he's been hurting his employees, then of course we'll do the right thing and hand that over to the police. But that doesn't absolve me from my responsibilities to protect his company. I'm not taking one side over the other."

She nodded, her expression guarded. "Have you considered the possibility that perhaps it was a crime of opportunity? Well...an almost crime of opportunity?"

"Yes, but that doesn't explain why this person managed to get into the gallery without tripping the alarm but couldn't get into the storage room."

She resumed painting, her movement slow and gentle behind the canvas. "No, I guess it doesn't. But I can tell you one thing, I am *not* romantically involved with Sean Ainslie. I may not be perfect, but I'm a one-man kind of woman."

One man. *Him.*

"Is that so?" Lord help him, but hearing those words made him feel all kinds of satisfied. "The bed was a lot emptier the other morning than I would have liked."

"Maybe you imagined the whole thing," she said softly.

"I don't think so, Wren. You know I'm not the creative type. I could never have dreamed up something that spectacular."

She bit down on her lip as she painted. "You might not be creative but you *are* good with your hands."

"So why the ninja exit in the middle of the night?"

"I didn't want the morning to be awkward."

He chuckled. "It would have been many things, but awkward isn't one of them."

"How can you be sure?" Her voice sounded so small, so vulnerable.

Hidden by the canvas, she continued to paint. Something told him paintings were her shield, a way for her to express herself that didn't require words.

"Because I had an amazing time and I was hoping it might continue. I think we work well together and there's nothing awkward about that."

"But we're so different." She put down her brush and stepped out from behind the easel. "You're the perfect specimen of adulthood and I'm…not."

"I was hoping after all we'd shared that my maturity wouldn't be the thing you focused on." He pushed up from his chair and walked over to her.

"It's not, but you're so perfect at everything." She laughed. "It's kind of intimidating."

"I'm *not* perfect at everything."

Her arms folded across her chest, propping up her bust so that his eyes were drawn there. The white tank top was splattered with paint. "Oh yeah? Tell me something you're bad at."

"Relaxing." He held up a hand when she rolled her eyes. "Hear me out. I go crazy on the weekends if I don't have anything to do. Since I met you, I've actually had a meal without working while I was eating."

"I'm not sure that counts."

"Okay." The challenge was most definitely accepted. "I suck at keeping plants alive, I can't make out the difference between expensive wine and cheap wine. I'm an embarrassingly terrible poker player and I was told once by an ex that I give really painful massages."

Wren laughed. "I don't know which of those is my favorite."

"I've never given a massage to anyone since that conversation. It's my secret shame."

"I don't believe it for a second." She reached out for his hand and rubbed her thumb over the center of his palm. "Your hands were good to me the other night."

The small touch sent excitement rocketing through him. All Wren had to do was get close and his body lit up like a fireworks display. Normally, he was able to keep his attraction to women contained, controlled. But with Wren, everything he normally held dear seemed to fly out the window.

"I'm happy to hear it," he said.

"Want to see how the painting is going?" she asked, her voice soft and low.

Knowing how cagey Wren had been about showing him her paintings the night they'd first had dinner together, this show of trust warmed him. "Definitely."

She slipped her fingers between his and tugged him

closer to the easel. "It's nowhere near finished. But having you here really helped me to get in the zone."

"Must be my type A personality rubbing off on you."

"Maybe."

From the first version he'd seen, this was leaps and bounds ahead. The lines were filled in; his eyes seemed dark and intense. She'd shaped his mouth to have an almost imperceptible lift at their corners, like they were sharing a private joke as she painted.

"It's incredible," he said. "You're incredible."

Viewing himself through her eyes, he wasn't invisible. He wasn't second best. He wasn't the boy who'd struggled to belong. She saw him for who he really was. He couldn't let that go, no matter how much his sensible side told him to walk away from this woman.

She wasn't planning to stay, so falling for her was a bad idea. He'd be setting himself up for disappointment. But that was before they'd started to explore the chemistry between them.

What if she had a reason to stay?

8

WREN MIGHT BE the impulsive type, but even she could see that getting involved with Rhys was a dumb idea.

His security company was making headway with their investigation. They'd already figured out that Sean was crossing the line with his employees—how much longer would it take before Rhys figured out her reason for being at the gallery?

My personal feelings on the situation don't matter.

His words danced in her head. It was clear that once he found out the truth, he'd still think her in the wrong, even with her good intentions. Which meant it was one thing to indulge in a night of passion, but it was quite another to go back for seconds.

But that was the problem with Rhys—she couldn't get enough. She couldn't keep her distance. She didn't *want* to.

"We have something here," he said. "I'm not sure what it is, but I can't ignore it."

"You know I'm not going to be staying after my internship is over," she said, as though it might shake her brain into action. How could she explore these burgeoning feelings for him while at the same time lying to him? She couldn't.

But sex was something she could keep separate from her emotions. If she drew a line between the two, maybe she could have it all.

"Is that set in stone?" He searched her face, his own expression unreadable.

"I have to get back to my family," she said. "Besides, if I stayed I would inevitably make your life messy and disorganized."

He pulled her against him, his large hands cupping her face and tilting her up to him. "Maybe you can teach me to be messy while you're here."

Relief swam through her. She couldn't promise anything, nor could she allow herself to get emotionally entangled with him. But that didn't mean she was ready to give up the incredible feeling of his hands on her.

"You couldn't handle it," she teased.

The graze of his lips across her jaw sent a shiver racing down her spine. "Try me, Wren. I dare you."

"You dare me, huh? I don't back down from dares."

"I was hoping you'd say that." His mouth captured hers for one blissful second. One all-consuming, earth-shattering moment.

It was wrong, she knew that. Wrong to kiss him while she was keeping secrets from him, wrong to allow him to touch her even though their goals were in direct competition. But her body overrode her sensibilities.

"You're on," she said, pulling away.

She ordered him to sit as she went into the kitchen.

The man had no idea what he'd started. Anyone from her hometown would know not to dare her unless they expected to suffer the consequences. Once, in high school, she'd gotten herself suspended for letting a duck loose in the library on Kylie's challenge.

Grinning to herself, she pulled a jar of chocolate sauce from the cupboard and found a small paint brush. The sauce had been intended to go with the brownies, but now she had a much better use for it.

"Should I be nervous?" Rhys asked in a way that sounded anything but.

"No, but you might want to take your top off." She sauntered back to where he sat, being sure to swing her hips.

"Is that what I think it is?" He eyed the sauce and divested himself of his T-shirt.

"We're going to have a little painting lesson," she said, ignoring his question.

With languid slowness, she drew down the zipper on her shorts. She was urged on by the catch in Rhys's breath as she shimmed out of the denim. It would be so easy to become addicted to the way he reacted to her, as though she were the sexiest thing he'd ever laid eyes on.

Under his heated gaze, she might be able to believe it.

"Ready to get messy?" she asked with a grin.

"You'd better not be teasing," he growled. "If we're going to do this, I want to do it properly."

"Of course you do." She set the tub of chocolate sauce down and dipped the brush into it. "Mr. Perfect doesn't do things by halves, does he?"

"No, he doesn't."

The brush dripped with sticky, chocolaty goodness. "Last chance to back out."

"Not a fucking chance, Wren." His eyes met hers, his pupils wide and his breathing ragged.

She climbed into his lap, sauce in one hand and her

brush in the other. The hard ridge of his erection pressed against the inside of her bare leg and she made sure to wriggle enough to elicit a groan from him.

Power surged through her body. She'd never felt like this before, so in control and fiercely sexy. It made her whole body pulse with desire.

"You're all mine now," she whispered as she streaked the chocolate across his chest. "All dirty and all mine."

Another streak followed, and this time she chased the brush with her tongue, catching a flat, dark nipple between her lips. A low, guttural sound emanated from within him as he ground up against her, his hands flying to her hips.

"You like that?" she teased.

The brush peppered his skin with sticky marks, her tongue smudging and swirling the chocolate around. She used her teeth, her lips and her hands to mark him. To claim him.

"Don't think you're the only one who gets to have fun," he said, thrusting his hands into her hair as he pulled her in for a searing, chocolaty kiss.

Her lips were sticky with sauce and it melded perfectly with the taste of him. "I'm the artist here."

His hands were under her tank top, her breasts spilling into his palm. With a rough flick of his thumb, her sex clenched so tight that her breath stuttered. She pressed against him to alleviate the pressure, but it only made her want him more.

"Damn," he muttered as he kissed his way down her neck, almost knocking the jar out of her hand. "We need to get you naked."

"My hands are full. You'll have to help me out."

She'd expected him to pull the fabric over her head,

but instead he grabbed the tank top at the neckline and ripped the whole thing open. The sound of cotton tearing pulled a shocked laugh from her, which dissolved into a heady groan as his mouth came down to her chest.

"Yes," he breathed, snaking one hand around her waist as he sat back and raked his eyes over her.

Dipping the brush into the sauce again, she let the chocolate drizzle over her now-exposed chest. Anything to make him put his mouth on her again.

"You're going to have us both covered in this stuff," he said before dipping his head.

"That's the plan."

Her head rolled back as he took one nipple between his lips, alternating between sucking and flicking his tongue over the sensitive bud. The moment he used his teeth on her—so gentle and yet not quite—her eyes fluttered shut.

His arm around her waist, strong and sure, kept her from melting to the ground. She wasn't sure if she could come from simply having his mouth on her breast, but the pleasure spiking hard and fast inside her said it was indeed a possibility. Her whole body tensed and ached for him; it responded to his every touch as though he'd been doing it for years. As though he'd written her instruction manual.

"You taste so good," he moaned between her breasts, nuzzling them and nipping at the tender flesh there. "And not just from the chocolate."

The spot between her legs throbbed, and she rocked against him, the friction making stars dance before her eyes. She needed him inside her. Soon.

"There's somewhere else I want to taste." He looked up, his eyes black with arousal.

Feeling bold, she got a little more sauce onto the brush

and carefully placed the jar on the ground. "Your turn to be Picasso."

With a wicked grin, he took the brush from her and stood, supporting her weight with one arm. The torn tank slipped down her shoulders, and she shrugged it off. Thank god she hadn't bothered with a bra.

"I can't do my best work in this cramped position," he said. "I want to be able to see all of you."

Before she could figure out where he was taking her, he'd placed her softly down on the kitchen table. His gentleness totally belied the rough edge in his voice and the raw excitement on his face.

Tucking a finger into the waistband of her panties, he dragged them down her legs.

STANDING IN FRONT of Wren, her body laid out like a feast, he felt as mighty as a god. There was something about her responsiveness that filled him with heady, primal power. With her, he could do anything. Be anything.

Right now he wanted to be the man to bring her pleasure.

"Ready for a taste of your own medicine?" he asked, pushing her legs apart with his hand.

Her teeth dented her lower lip and she nodded. "Yes."

Dragging the brush from her belly button down to the bare patch of skin at the apex of her thighs, he forced himself to move slowly. This wasn't something that could—or should—be rushed. He would draw her pleasure out, string her along as much as willpower would allow.

The streak of dark chocolate against her white skin was striking and erotic. He circled the brush lower, creating a swirl over the lips of her sex. When he stroked her clit with the brush, she gasped and arched her back. Her slim fingers curled around the edge of the table, and it was all he could do not to guide them to his steel-hard cock.

Patience. He would have his turn soon, but not before he tasted her.

The brush caressed her skin as he painted her, concentrating on the bundle of nerves between her legs. A low, throaty moan was his reward.

"Please, Rhys," she gasped. "Oh God, please."

"I thought art was supposed to take time," he teased. "You can't rush a masterpiece."

Her hips bucked as he applied more pressure, her lashes fluttering. He'd never seen a more beautiful sight.

"This masterpiece is about to combust," she said through gritted teeth.

A chuckle rumbled deep in his chest. "I'd better take care of that."

At the first swipe of his tongue she let out a low, keening moan. He took his time, cleaning her up with his tongue until there wasn't a trace of the chocolate sauce left. His lips peppered her with soft kisses as he worked his way around her, avoiding the one spot where she wanted him most.

She grasped his head, seeking to control his movements. "Please, Rhys. I'm dying."

"No, you're not." He nuzzled her. "I'll look after you."

Running his hands up and down her thighs, he parted her with his thumbs. She was swollen with desire, her body totally primed and ready for him. The sight made all the blood in his body rush south, leaving him lightheaded in the best way possible.

"I need to come," she whimpered.

Her pleas turned into a low groan of surrender as he drew her clit between his lips, focusing on that one sensitive spot until the shudders started. Her thigh trembled against his cheek and her breath quickened. When the moment of her release hit, her nails dug into his shoulders and she cried out his name.

He'd never forget how it sounded on her lips.

Gathering her up in his arms, he carried her to the bathroom. Her arms wound around his neck as if out of instinct. "Where are you taking me?"

"You've had your fun. Now I'm going to clean us up," he said, pressing a kiss to her forehead.

"See, I knew you couldn't handle being messy."

"I don't think you'll be complaining once we get started."

Her bathroom was the same as the one in his apartment, at least when it came to the layout and fittings. But instead of his fluffy gray towels hanging from the rack, she had threadbare versions in an almost psychedelic pink-and-green print. The top of her sink was dotted with several tubes of lip gloss, a hairbrush and a bottle of perfume. A pair of hot-pink panties sat in one corner on the floor.

"Don't judge me," she grumbled as he set her down, shoving the panties to one side with her foot.

"No judgment. Why don't you get the water running and I'll get out of these pants?"

Her eyes sparkled. "Good idea."

She stepped into the shower and turned on the tap. Water ran down her body and she jumped up and down on the spot while it warmed up. The cold spray made her nipples pink and stiff.

For a moment all he could do was stare. As steam

started to billow up, she tilted her head back and let the spray of water slide down her. It mixed with the chocolate on her chest and ran down her body, washing away the evidence of their messy interlude.

"You're supposed to be stripping," she said, pointing to his jeans. "Come on, I've shown you mine."

His cock was straining hard against the fly of his jeans, and he gave in to the desire for some friction there. Rubbing the heel of his palm up and down the hard length, he watched as Wren's eyes widened. He loosened his belt and unzipped the denim, letting it drop to his feet. As he pushed down his boxer briefs, he felt her eyes on him.

They were hungry eyes. Excited eyes. The kind of eyes that made him feel alive.

"Like what you see?" he asked as she drank him in.

Her head bobbed. "Yeah."

He kicked the discarded clothing to one side and joined her in the shower. The warm water loosened muscles he hadn't realized were bunched up. He'd been coiled like a spring waiting to have his moment with her.

"You don't have to stop at looking," he said, cornering her against the tiled wall.

"That might get messy," she warned.

"I'm coming around to your way of doing things." He bent his head to hers and claimed her in a scorching kiss. "I can handle a little mess with you."

There was no hesitation when she reached for him, her fingers wrapping around his cock as though they belonged there. She squeezed him and ran her hand up and down, twisting her wrist slightly. Feeling him. Learning him.

"Is that good?" she asked, her voice breathy.

"Hell yeah." He reached for her free hand and guided her to cup his balls. "This feels good, too."

Her curiosity was like a drug and her touch moved from tentative to bold. Stoking harder, she rubbed the tip of him between her legs.

"Jesus, Wren. What are you doing to me?"

"Something right by the sound of it."

He jerked into her grip, his hips bucking of their own accord. There was only one way this could end, and that end would be pretty damn sudden if he didn't take back control. "Tell me you bought some protection."

"Oops."

"Wren," he growled. If they had to stop now the frustration may kill him.

"It's okay." She pressed a finger to his lips. "Let me take care of it."

She sank to her knees, her hands running down over his stomach to his thighs. Bracing herself against him, she dropped her head to the tip of his cock. Her tongue darted out to taste him. Test him.

It was sweet, sweet torture.

She guided his hand to her hair, and he threaded his fingers through the now wet strands. When she sank her mouth onto him, he groaned and the sound vibrated within the confines of the shower. There was nothing more erotic than watching himself slide in and out of her pink lips. Or the way she wrapped her fingers around him, working him slowly to orgasm.

She drew back, releasing him from her mouth. "You taste good."

"You feel good." He rested his head against the tiles, relishing the consistent stroke of her hand. "Those lips are incredible."

"Just my lips?" Her tongue swirled around the sensitive crown of his cock.

"That, too." The words were strangled by his pleasure. "Everything, Wren. So. Damn. Good."

She guided him back into her mouth and hummed in response. The vibrations almost sent him over the edge, and he fisted his hand in her hair. She scraped her teeth gently along the underside of his cock, ratcheting up the sensation.

"Wren." His hips jerked as she sank down farther, taking him as far as she could.

A tight ache balled up inside him as she sucked, and she flicked her tongue over the sensitive head until his thighs twitched. Release washed over him. He let her name fall from his lips over and over and over as he emptied himself inside her.

A moment later she was wrapped up in his arms, and they stayed there until the water turned cold and goose bumps broke out on her skin. It would have been easy to stay there forever.

Why do you always have to leap to forever? She's spelled it out for you already. She's not *going to stay.*

But he shoved the thoughts aside, wanting his worries to disappear like the water down her drain. He couldn't let go of the idea that their bond went far beyond mind-bending pleasure and into something more emotional. More real. All he had to do was convince her to give them a shot.

9

AFTER THEIR SHOWER, Rhys took Wren to his place. They didn't want to fall victim to a lack of condoms again, and it wasn't long before they wound up on his bed in a tangled heap of limbs. She'd lost count of the number of times he'd made her body soar.

It was a new experience for her, this contentment and trust that she had with Rhys. Sure, he teased her about her messy, disorganized lifestyle—and she gave it back to him—but that kind of teasing had an inherent sense of familiarity. In fact, she felt more at home in his arms than she ever had in Charity Springs.

It would be hard to say goodbye to him, but she couldn't forget about the people who needed her back home.

With her cheek pressed against his rib cage, the slow rhythm of his breathing soothed her. Her fingertips gently traced the dark trail of hair that ran from his belly button to underneath the white bedsheet. Even after what they'd done, he was still semi-hard, his length tenting the sheet.

"Go on, I don't bite," he said, his voice husky. "You can touch me."

"I thought you were sleeping." She tilted her face up

to his and kissed him. His tongue moved against hers with a lazy confidence that made her whole body tingle.

"Hard to sleep with a beautiful girl getting handsy with me."

"I can stop."

He brushed her hair back from her forehead. "Don't you dare."

But just then her stomach grumbled. Outside, the sun had started to dip and rich gold beams of light filtered through her blinds.

"I forgot to have lunch today," she said. "I guess brownies and chocolate sauce don't make for a very good meal replacement."

"Want to order in?"

A happy bubble expanded in her chest. "It's like you can read my mind."

"Let me get it." He pushed up from the bed and pulled the sheet over her.

Within the hour they were curled up on his couch, eating Chinese food.

"I can't believe you don't like fried rice," she said, tucking into her chow mein. "And don't even get me started on the tofu."

"My body is a finely tuned athletic machine," he said, but he couldn't keep a straight face. "I've never had as many empty calories as I did this afternoon."

"Those calories were one hundred percent delicious and worth it."

"Agreed." He dug around in the container with his chopsticks. "But I do take nutrition seriously."

"You take *everything* seriously."

"It's a product of my upbringing, I guess." He popped a piece of chicken into his mouth and chewed.

At the mention of his past, his face hardened. The warmth in his eyes dulled and small tension lines formed at the corners of his mouth.

"How so?"

"I guess I thought that if I became the perfect son then my mother would love me again," he said. "I studied my ass off. I ate whatever crazy green shit she put on my plate. I never talked back, never broke a rule."

Her heart bled for him. She knew how hard it was to be the "other" child, to always be second place. Only her relegation to the back of the line was because of her disappointing lack of focus, rather than grief. Still, the reason didn't matter so much as the outcome. She understood his pain.

"I even quit basketball," he continued, staring straight ahead, his face rigid. "I would have given up anything."

"But it didn't work?"

"No. I was too much my father for her to ever see me as a separate person. And when I told her that I wanted to go into the police force, she flipped." He snorted. "I don't know why she was so worried. It wasn't like she even seemed to enjoy my presence half the time."

"Why didn't she want you to become a police officer?"

"That's how my dad died. He crashed his car while chasing a guy who was fleeing the scene of a drug bust." He looked at her, and some of the warmth crept back into his eyes. "He was a complete hero. I wanted to be just like him."

"But your mom thought it was too risky?"

"Yeah. Nothing I could say would make her change her mind. Eventually she said if I chose to live that kind of life then she'd have nothing to do with me." Pain streaked across his face but it was gone as quickly as it had appeared. "So I went to college and studied technology instead."

"That's sad that you didn't get to pursue your dream." She put her food aside and scooted along the couch to be close to him. She couldn't ease his pain but she wanted to try, nonetheless. "I'm sure your father would be proud of you, even if you didn't follow in his footsteps."

"I'd like to think that." He fished out the last piece of chicken from his dinner and placed the empty container on the coffee table. "And I'm happy with my career now. I'm doing what I'm meant to be doing. I'm good at my job and it's the one area of my life where I can score a touchdown or two."

His self-deprecating smile tore her heart into pieces. It wasn't only that she'd come to respect Rhys deeply. He was kindhearted, giving and—despite his slight obsession with tidiness—wonderfully accepting of who she was.

Would he be so accepting if he knew why you were here? Not likely.

"I'm not sure what *you* would call it, but I'm certain we scored a touchdown before," she said, swallowing back her guilt.

She wanted to trust him, wanted it deep down to her bones because she sensed he was different. That he wouldn't turn on her like Christian had. But this wasn't only her secret. It was Kylie's, too. And knowing that Rhys was such a stand-up guy meant there was a chance he would turn her in, even if he didn't want to. And that would end all hope of finding out what had really happened to Kylie.

"Good team effort," he replied with a grin as he

draped an arm around her shoulder. "And it was definitely two touchdowns."

"Not that you're counting."

"I like knowing you're satisfied." His voice was deep and growly against her ear. "I don't want you to go home with the feeling that I left you hanging."

"No chance of that. And I do appreciate it." She rested her head against his shoulder and relaxed into him. "My ex wasn't really the giving type."

"Is that why he's an ex?"

"No." Her hands instinctively curled into fists like they always did when she thought about what Christian had done to her.

The worst part of his betrayal was that she'd been stupid enough to allow it to happen. She'd been totally blind to his flaws until it was too late. Christian's deluded sense of self-righteousness and self-importance had jumped up and bit her in the ass.

"Our sex life wasn't the reason we broke up, but it certainly wasn't a positive part of our relationship," she said, shoving aside her bitterness. "Too many guilty feelings."

"Guilty feelings?" Rhys raised a dark brow. "Why the hell would you feel guilty for having sex?"

She shook her head. "The people in our town are conservative, and they have a pretty screwed-up view of women and sex. Apparently, we should do it to keep our men happy but we shouldn't enjoy it too much."

"I don't even know what to say to that." He shook his head. "That's messed up."

"Yeah, it is." She bobbed her head.

"I'm surprised you want to go back to that."

"There are people there I care about. My sister is there. My best friend…she needs me."

"That might be so, but what do *you* need?"

She blinked. "What do you mean?"

"It's not a trick question." He chuckled. "If you didn't have to worry about anyone else, what would you do?"

Wren sucked on her bottom lip and grappled for an answer. It shouldn't be so hard to come up with a "perfect life scenario," but for some reason she found herself tongue-tied. Perhaps it was because part of her had given up on the idea of being an artist…but without that she was no longer sure of who she was.

"How about living on a remote island with magical Wi-Fi and an endless supply of brownies?" she said with a glib shrug.

"I'm not buying that."

"Honestly, I don't know what I want right now." She nestled her head into his shoulder again and breathed in the faint scent of soap on his skin. "All I know is that after the internship I have to go back home."

"Because your friend needs you? Surely she would understand that you've got to live your own life."

"Something bad happened to her."

The truth hovered on her tongue, but she couldn't bring herself to ruin the perfect bubble of comfort that surrounded her and Rhys. For the first time in months she was happy and wanted.

As soon as I have something on Sean, she promised herself. *Then I'll come clean.*

If she came to Rhys with proof, it would soften the blow and help to show him that she hadn't intended to deceive him. Only to help her friend.

"She's not doing great." Wren swallowed against the emotion rising up her throat. "She's lost all the joy in her life and she's not eating. I'm afraid for her, and she doesn't have anyone else."

"That's very noble of you." His fingertips traced circles on her bare arm. "But she'll get over this rough patch, and you have to put yourself first at some point."

"Yeah, I know." If only she could figure out what putting herself first actually meant.

"I'm happy to help you forget about home for a while longer." He traced the gentle circles lower and lower until he'd found the sensitive skin of her inner thigh. His touch held promises of pleasure to come.

"I'm happy to let you."

His fingers brushed higher, skating under the edge of her shorts and grazing her panties. "Does that mean you won't sneak out on me tonight?"

"Presumptuous," she teased. "Who said I was staying the night?"

The pressure of his touch intensified as he slipped a finger beneath her panties. A moan escaped her lips before she could stop it. Damn Rhys and his talented hands. She had no chance of hiding how she felt *or* what she wanted.

"You're free to go at any time." He let out a cocky chuckle as she arched against his hand.

"I guess I could stay awhile." Her eyes clamped shut as he found her sweet spot. "Since you're being so persuasive."

"Glad to see my plan is working."

Wren's mind went blank as he eased her back on the couch. For now, she wanted to lose herself in his touch. She could deal with her conflicted feelings tomorrow.

BY THE TIME Monday rolled around, Wren had yet to find clarity on her situation. She'd disentangled herself from Rhys on Saturday morning, intending to leave, but then he'd kissed her and somehow they'd ended up having breakfast together.

She'd made a point of leaving before lunch, because she needed space to think. But by Sunday she was craving him again and she'd knocked on his door with an offer of dinner and a movie. They'd made love on his couch, their bodies working so perfectly together that Wren almost forget why she'd come to New York.

Wren dragged herself out of her reverie as voices floated down the gallery hall. Lola's soft Southern twang was instantly recognizable, as was a harsher New York accent. As they came closer, Wren caught snatches of their conversation.

"Sean will be with you shortly, but if you want to have a chat with Wren, she's in here." Lola appeared in the doorway to the studio with two people. "Wren, you remember Quinn Dellinger from Cobalt & Dane? And this is her colleague, Owen Fletcher. They're supervising the installation of the new cameras today."

She left her station to shake their hands. "Hello."

Quinn's sharp hazel eyes darted around the room. "We wanted to give you a heads-up to watch out for our guys. They'll have ladders and wires all over the place, so step carefully. We don't want anyone getting injured."

Could this mean the storage room would be open? Maybe this was her opportunity to see what was inside. Wren forced her expression to remain neutral. "Thanks."

At that moment Sean poked his head into the room. "I trust you have something to work on," he said to her, his cold stare making her step back instinctively.

"Yes, I do."

She'd realized at some point over the weekend that giving Ainslie a painting with Rhys's face probably wasn't the smartest move. Apart from the obvious risk of Sean recognizing Rhys and wondering why Wren had chosen to paint him, there was something preventing her from parting with it. It wasn't yet finished, but her Muse had reappeared. She'd even found herself thinking about new paintings and wanting to reach for her brushes. There was that itch in her fingertips, creative desire slowly igniting inside her like a flame resurrected from the very last ember.

But that left her with a problem. Sean's ultimatum. She needed a painting and she needed it quickly. So Wren had gone back to her passion and painted a woman. Her sister.

"Good, because you owe me a painting this week and I don't want you to bother the team while they're working."

"I understand, I'm working on something new for you."

Over the next hour, Wren forced herself to work quickly while the Cobalt & Dane team started the installation. A technician, accompanied by Owen, was installing a camera right outside the studio. Wren used the opportunity to excuse herself under the guise of going to the restroom.

Instead, Wren inched along the hallway toward the storage room. Quinn was in there, talking to someone. Was it Sean? She was sure he'd mentioned having an appointment today. This could be her one and only chance to get inside.

She could only hear Quinn's side of the conversation; she must be on the phone. Wren gathered her long skirt in one hand to stop it from brushing along the floor as she tiptoed along.

"The installation is going well," Quinn said. "We're fitting the last group of cameras, but we'll have to configure the software because the client has a few customizations. Yeah…" Pause. "Well, I *could* come on my own if you would sign off on this damn training."

She must be talking to Rhys. Wren flattened her back to the wall just outside the storage room and strained to hear if anyone else was inside.

Nothing.

Sucking in a breath, she moved closer and leaned forward to take a peek into the room. At that moment Sean Ainslie came out, a dark expression on his face.

"Are you looking for me, Wren? I thought you had work to keep you busy." He folded his arms across his chest. He was a lot more built than she'd first guessed. His fitted T-shirt exposed a gym-honed body. But instead of all that physical power appealing to her, it made her feel ill.

"I, uh…yes, actually. I wanted guidance on my painting," she lied. "I realize you're busy but I had a burst of inspiration and I would really appreciate your expertise."

"You know the rules about the storage room, Wren," he said, but his expression had lost its edge.

"I'm sorry, I didn't even think…"

"It's fine. Let's take a look at this painting."

Nodding, Wren stifled a sigh of relief. She'd weaseled her way out of trouble this time…but she may not get a second chance. Perhaps Rhys would be able to access the cameras to check inside. She made a mental note to suss out whether he would do that once the installation was complete.

REALITY HAD BURST the happy bubble that was Rhys's weekend. Monday had flown past in a blur of meetings and he hadn't left the office until 9:00 p.m. Tempted as he'd been to call Wren on his way home, he didn't want her to get the impression that she was a booty call...as much as her booty had *definitely* been on his mind.

The next day, he was sitting at his desk, wondering where his Tuesday had gotten to when Quinn and Owen arrived to give an update on Ainslie Ave.

"How'd the installation go?" he asked, dragging his focus back to work.

"Good." Quinn took a seat on the other side of Rhys's desk. "We're currently working through the customization requirements for the monitoring system."

"Has anything else come up?"

Owen raked a hand through his blond hair. "I managed to speak with the interns after we finished up for the day. They all seemed a little cagey about answering questions, particularly where Sean was involved."

"So no confirmation that he's sleeping with any of them?" Rhys remembered Wren's admission about Aimee.

"Not a thing."

Interesting. Either Aimee had lied to Quinn or she'd lied to Wren.

What if Wren lied to you?

He shoved the thought aside immediately. What reason would Wren have to lie to him? If something really was going on between Sean Ainslie and Aimee, perhaps the other woman had a reason for keeping it quiet. A reason she wouldn't feel comfortable sharing with a security company.

"I had some luck with the gallery's ex-employees, though," Quinn said.

After a few minutes detailing her calls to several former Ainslie Ave employees, she got to the one that she was most excited about. "I spoke with a woman named

Kylie Samuels. She worked at the gallery until six months ago when she returned to her home in Charity Springs, Idaho."

The name of the town rang a bell, but Rhys couldn't place where he'd heard it before. "What's the significance of that?"

"Well, I did some research and it barely has seven hundred residents." She paused as if for dramatic effect. "And guess who *also* happens to come from Charity Springs? Wren Livingston."

Rhys tried not to let the surprise show on his face. Why wouldn't she have mentioned that someone from her hometown had also worked for Ainslie Ave? Perhaps it hadn't occurred to her. Or maybe she didn't know this Kylie Samuels. Though that *did* seem unlikely for a town of such a small size.

"Any signs they're connected to one another?" he asked.

"I assumed you wouldn't be satisfied with circumstantial evidence," Quinn replied with a smile that made her look like the cat who'd got the cream. "They both attended the local high school and I found a picture of them from a fund-raising event."

She pulled up the photo on her laptop. It seemed to be several years old and showed two girls with their arms wrapped around one another's shoulders. Wren's ear-to-ear grin struck something in his chest. She looked so much more at ease in this picture, so free and innocent. Her hair was shorter and her face was painted with big blue flowers, making her resemble some kind of fairy or nymph.

"That's Wren Livingston," Owen said, pointing with his pen. He was oblivious to the fact that Rhys knew her face intimately, and now her body, as well. "And this is Kylie Samuels."

They could have been sisters. Kylie had blond hair, too, though it was a few shades darker than Wren's. And she was smaller. Skinny rather than slender. They wore the same breezy smiles and crazy face paint.

"What did Kylie have to say?" Rhys asked.

"She really didn't want to talk to me," Quinn said. "But I managed to get out of her that she ended the internship early because of a clash with Ainslie. She said it was something to do with her paintings, but when I pressed her she clammed up."

"Did you ask her about whether or not she was friends with Wren?"

Quinn huffed. "Barely. The second I mentioned Wren's name, Kylie said something about having an appointment and then she hung up on me. I've been trying to call her back since late last week to get more information, but she won't take my calls."

For the first time Rhys felt guilty for skirting the lines of appropriateness by sleeping with Wren. Up till now, it hadn't bothered him too much because he'd seen no reason why she would be involved in the security breaches. But this information about her friend shed some new light on the situation. It created a link where there hadn't been one previously.

Was it possible that she'd been lying to him this whole time?

"Keep chasing the ex-employees," Rhys said. "See what else you can dig up. But we have to continue servicing Ainslie as a client."

Rhys called an end to the meeting but asked Owen to stay behind. As much as he trusted Quinn, she had a fiery personality, and once she decided that she didn't like someone, her mind was hard to change. He needed a more balanced opinion.

"I want your take on this," he said, running a hand over his closely cropped hair. "I get something seems off about this guy, but surely he wouldn't have called us in if he had something to hide."

"I have seen stranger things in this line of work," Owen replied with a wry smile. "There's definitely something going on. He seemed resistant to the cameras, and I'm not buying the line about him not wanting to monitor his staff."

"Me, either."

"The external security is also pretty strong. He's got a monitored system that they set every night, which notifies him if there are multiple unsuccessful attempts on the pin code at either the front door or the entrance in the loading dock. If the alarm is tripped, then it notifies our call center and we dispatch someone to check it out. But…" Owen paused, rubbing a hand along his jaw. "There were no external security cameras until yesterday. Not even for the loading area behind the gallery. That's strange."

"How did things go with the tech side of things?"

"Quinn is handling that, since that's more her forte than mine. She's still making her way through the email logs, but it does look like someone used Ainslie's log-in on the interns' terminal in the studio."

"Is it possible Ainslie needed to access his email while he was in that room?"

"Sure, it's definitely possible. But we're going to correlate the log-in time stamp with activity on his account to see if anything strange is going on."

"Okay, I want an update as soon as possible."

"You're getting quite involved in this case," Owen commented. "I thought you were supposed to be the big-picture guy."

He was. Rhys's role didn't require him to get involved in individual assignments beyond the initial approach and ensuring his staff were keeping to schedule. And since the tech security part of the Cobalt & Dane business was growing quickly, he really didn't have time to dive deep into the details. Senior security consultants—like Owen—were the ones managing such things.

It occurred to him that maybe Owen thought he was overstepping.

Rhys cleared his throat. "This is the first assignment that Quinn is leading and I want to make sure she's fully supported."

The lie was sour in his mouth. This wasn't like him at all; normally he was Mr. By The Book. Now he was keeping things from his team and had possibly crossed a line with Wren.

He'd speak to her tonight, get them both on the same page. He couldn't break any more rules now that there was a chance she was involved.

10

WREN NARROWED HER eyes at the half-done canvas in front of her. It had started out a mess but the vision was finally beginning to come through. Her deadline to deliver a painting to Sean was drawing near and she finally felt confident that she'd have something to hand in.

Wren softened Debbie's blond hair with a fan brush. She stroked the painting as if combing the hair, merging some of the brassier tones into the pale, light-reflecting sections until the color looked seamless and natural.

She lost herself in the image until her phone buzzed. Kylie's face flashed up on the screen like a ghost arriving to haunt her. It was the third time she'd called today.

"Aren't you going to get that?" Aimee asked as she turned away from her canvas. "Or are you avoiding someone?"

"I'm not avoiding anyone," Wren replied. "I'm simply trying to find the right moment to talk."

It wasn't untrue. Wren had to keep up the ruse with her friend that she was on an art retreat that restricted mobile phone usage. That meant she would call Kylie back at the time they'd agreed on over email.

Why would she be calling early? Maybe the security company called her again.

"I hate cell phones," Aimee said. "People just expect you to drop everything to take a call and if you don't message back quick enough…watch out."

She was still wearing longer sleeves but she appeared to have forgiven Sean, if the goo-goo eyes she'd given him that morning were anything to go on.

"How's the arm?" Wren asked as she continued working on Debbie's hair.

"Oh fine, it's nothing too bad. I, uh… I overreacted the other day." Her voice sounded cheerful on the surface, but there was something hollow beneath it. A false confidence that Wren knew all too well.

Her voice had been the same when she'd covered up for Christian with Debbie or her other friends. It was the sound of backpedaling.

"You didn't overreact." Wren looked up.

"It was an accident."

"Bruises like that *aren't* an accident."

Aimee refocused on her painting. "I don't want you to get involved."

"Then why did you tell me about it? If he's hurting you—"

"He's not." She swiped her hands through her long gold hair. "I don't know. I was having a rough day… It's nothing."

"It's *not* nothing."

At that moment footsteps cut through the quiet of the gallery and Sean walked in, a small canvas tucked under one arm. "What's going on?"

"Just working," Wren replied, keeping her face as neutral as possible. Her body seemed to tense whenever he was around.

Aimee's eyes had dropped to floor. Something about the way she avoided his gaze didn't feel right to Wren. Aimee's bottom lip was drawn tight between her teeth. Sean whispered something in her ear and she nodded, her expression blank.

"Enough talking," Sean said to them both. "If you're in need of *more* work, the kitchen could use a clean."

As he walked away Wren caught a glimpse of the canvas he was carrying. The bold streaks of orange and teal seemed familiar, but her mind couldn't place where she'd seen it. Before she could get a closer look, he was gone.

"Please don't ask me about it again," Aimee said with a heavy sigh. "Okay? It's none of your business."

She walked out of the room, leaving Wren alone with her thoughts. When her phone started buzzing, Kylie's smiling face flashing up again, she answered it.

"Hey. Sorry I couldn't answer before, I—"

"Don't you dare tell me that you're at an art retreat, Wren. Just don't." Kylie's anger radiated through the phone line. "I know you're at Ainslie Ave."

Shit. "I can explain—"

"What the hell were you thinking? I got out of there for a reason. Now you're on some secret vigilante mission and you refuse to take my calls." She sighed. "I had to find out from some damn security company who called me to check on Sean, and then when you wouldn't answer your phone…"

It's official, you're the worst friend in the world.

Standing up as quietly as she could, she tiptoed to the front of the gallery and slipped outside. "I'm sorry, I never wanted you to worry."

"How could I not? You don't know what an evil piece of shit Sean Ainslie is." Her voice wavered. "He's a monster, Wren. You need to come home. Now."

"I can't."

"Why not? What on earth do you think you're going to do?"

"I'm trying to figure out what he did to you, since you won't tell me. Then I'm going to get proof of it so we can go to the police."

"The police? Oh, Wren." Kylie let out a bitter laugh. "There is no proof. Ever wondered why there are no security cameras in that place and yet he keeps a giant room all locked up? That's because he doesn't want to leave any evidence."

"What did he do to you?"

"Apart from shattering an eye socket and fracturing my wrist?" The sound suddenly became muffled and Wren thought she could hear a faint sob.

"Just tell me. We can fix this."

"There is no 'we.' You're there, being stupid and acting without thinking—as usual—and I'm here. Broken and worrying about my best friend."

Wren winced at the sting of her friend's words. "What happened to you?"

"Please don't make me talk about it."

"Why? If he's done something so bad, shouldn't he be punished?"

"It's not worth it." Her words were strained, and Wren felt awful for putting her through this. But if she didn't push, Sean would keep hurting people. Like Aimee.

Kylie likely wasn't the first victim, and she sure as hell wasn't the last. Wren owed it to them both to put a stop to Ainslie's behavior.

She opened her mouth to argue, but the sight of a tall figure walking toward the gallery halted her speech. Late-afternoon light made Rhys's skin look even warmer and more touchable. His crisp white shirt revealed a V of skin at his neck and the sleeves were rolled back to expose strong forearms.

"We need to talk," he said.

WREN'S BLUE EYES WIDENED. For a moment she was silent. "Let's chat later," she said into the phone and ended the call. "I wasn't expecting to see you here today, Rhys. Is this official security business?"

"It is. Can you take a minute to talk?"

Her eyes darted to the door. "I was supposed to be starting my shift on the front desk in a few minutes."

"We can talk there."

A crease formed between her brows. "Sean doesn't like it if we're sitting around talking."

"He hired Cobalt & Dane to look into his security issues, so I'm sure he'll make an exception." He hated to be a hard-ass, but it would drive him crazy if he didn't get to the bottom of Wren's involvement with Sean Ainslie. "Shall we?"

She nodded and motioned for him to follow her inside. "Sure."

Today she wore a blue skirt that clung to the sweet curve of her hips and ass, accentuating her long lines. A paint-splattered apron sat over a white T-shirt that showed a hint of creamy skin without revealing too much.

But his mind could fill in the gaps. He knew how soft her shoulders were and how perfectly the swell of her breasts and the gentle indent at her waist filled his palms.

Stop it. This is business, and you're not laying a finger on her until you learn the truth.

"So, what can I help you with?" she asked as she removed her apron and stashed it away in a cupboard behind the desk.

"Do you know a Kylie Samuels?"

As the color drained from her face, Rhys realized he'd made a terrible mistake. Perhaps she was a lot better at hiding things than he'd given her credit for. Judging by her expression, Kylie Samuels was more than a simple acquaintance.

"Can we not talk about this here?" Her hands twisted in her lap.

"This is work, isn't it?"

"Please." Her eyes darted to the hallway that led to Ainslie's office. "I'll tell you everything, but I can't do it here."

Ice trickled through his veins at the hushed tone of her voice. He knew fear when he saw it. But he barricaded his sympathy deep inside. "What are you scared of?"

"There's more to Sean than he's letting on. Something bad is going on here, Rhys." She drew a deep breath. "And I'm scared I've screwed things up with you."

Why would she think she'd screwed things up with him if she'd simply forgotten to mention that someone she knew had worked here? It was an admission of guilt if he'd ever heard one.

"Please let me explain myself. Tonight—I'll make dinner," she said with a hopeful smile.

"Maybe we should go out." The farther away they were from any flat surfaces the safer it would be, since it was clear his self-control seemed to vanish around her.

He scribbled the address of a quiet diner not too far

from their walk-up. They'd be able to get a booth away from prying eyes and he wouldn't be tempted to let his body do the thinking for him if they were in a public place.

"Do you need to speak to Sean while you're here?" she asked. "I can call him out, if you'd like."

"No. Quinn and Owen will run Sean through the new monitoring system later. We've also got an update for him with the log-in reports."

"Find anything interesting?" she asked.

"I can't discuss that with you."

"Of course, I was just kidding," she said, but her eyes were suddenly guarded. Closed off.

In other words, message received.

He had to draw a line in the sand with her until he knew exactly where they stood. It had been wrong to assume Wren wasn't involved from the beginning. Naive, even. But that didn't mean he had to continue down that path. A mistake could be corrected at any point, and that's exactly what he would do now.

11

Rhys arrived at the diner early and procured them a booth. He'd been antsy all afternoon, unable to concentrate on the work he'd brought home. Unable to think about anything but how his carefree connection with Wren had become a career hazard. A potential liability.

Of course, he could be overacting. There might be a perfectly reasonable excuse for her not mentioning her friend's involvement with the gallery. Perhaps they'd drifted apart and were no longer friends. Or maybe she'd really believed that it wasn't worth bringing up.

Nothing wrong with being optimistic, but the rose-colored glasses are coming off now. Your number one priority is to get the facts.

The moment Wren walked into the diner heads turned in her direction. She was still in the fitted blue pencil skirt, but she'd swapped the T-shirt out for a black lace-trimmed camisole. The effect was mouthwatering. Appreciative eyes swept over Wren from all directions and Rhys found himself fighting back the urge to claim her with a kiss.

Facts first. Your lips don't go near her until you have what you need.

"Hi," she said almost shyly as she slipped into the seat across from him. A few wavy strands of blond hair had escaped her ponytail and framed her face.

In the intimate space of the booth, his senses were heightened. The accidental brush of her knee against his almost undid his resolve to keep his hands to himself.

"This is a cute place," she said. "I hope their burgers are good, I'm starving."

"This isn't a date, Wren."

Her lips pursed. "I know that, but thanks for making yourself clear. I'm still ordering food, though."

"I want to make sure we're on the same page," he said, signaling to a server. "This is work, nothing else."

"Got you loud and clear, Captain," she replied with more than a hint of sarcasm. "I bet you keep your employees on the straight and narrow."

"What's that supposed to mean?"

Her eyes remained on the menu. "You're a bit of a hard-ass when you're in work mode."

"Tough but fair, that's my motto."

"Yes, well, I'm sure that's fine at the office." She paused as the server took their orders. "But I'm not your employee."

He resisted the urge to ask her how she classified their relationship. It wasn't information that would help him right now. "So tell me how you know Kylie Samuels."

"Gee, you're not wasting any time, are you? Straight down to business." She poured water into both their glasses, her hands shaking ever so slightly. "She's an old friend. We grew up together."

"And you were aware that she'd interned for a brief period under Sean Ainslie?"

"Yes."

Wren's entire demeanor had changed—normally, she had this relaxed, fluidity to her movement. Now she appeared stiff and jerky. She wore an expression on her face that was so closed off, she may as well have been wearing a bag over her head.

"Do you know why she finished up her internship early?"

Her hands knotted in her lap. "Not exactly."

"I thought you were friends. It seems odd that she gave up an opportunity and returned home but didn't tell you why…and now you're here doing the exact same internship."

"She refused to explain why she came back. She wouldn't talk about it at all…" Her gaze was riveted on an imperfection in the table.

"Why do I feel like there's a 'but' coming?"

"When she came home, she was all beat up." Wren picked at the chipped laminate, her lips curling in anger. "She had a black eye, a busted eye socket, a broken wrist and bruises on her arms. Someone had really worked her over."

Rhys's stomach churned as he remembered the photos of Marguerite Bernard's swollen face. "But she wouldn't say who did it?"

"No. But it didn't take much to put two and two together. Anytime I mentioned the internship she either burst into tears or started yelling at me to keep quiet." When Wren finally looked up, Rhys saw a fire blazing in her eyes that was totally foreign. "I asked her if she'd gone to the police and she said no, because there was no proof."

"Is that why you're here?" The pieces of the puzzle started to click into place and Rhys didn't like the final image that was coming together.

"Yes."

"How did you get the internship?"

"Kylie and I had applied at the same time, but she got the job and I didn't." Her cheeks colored but she reset her shoulders. "Sean approached me after Kylie dropped out, and I thought it was the perfect opportunity to find out what had happened to her."

"Were you the one who tripped the security alert for the storage room?"

She looked him square in the eye, chin tilted slightly. "Yes."

"Have you accessed Sean Ainslie's emails by using his log-in credentials?"

Sucking on her lower lip, Wren appeared utterly torn. Her brows crinkled and she bounced her leg in an agitated rhythm beneath the table.

"I want you to be honest with me," he said.

"Yes. I accessed Sean's emails."

Shit. How on earth would he be able to explain that he'd been sleeping with the very person he'd been hired to catch? That he'd been too stupid and too naive to suspect her because she had an angelic face?

"Say something, Rhys," she said.

"Were you spending time with me because you wanted inside information?"

WREN FELT THE sting of his question down to the very marrow of her bones. "No, of course not."

Rhys sat like a hard, immovable lump of stone on the other side of the table. When the server arrived with their food a few minutes later, the young man looked awkwardly from one to the other. The tension must have been billowing from their table.

She'd just admitted to accessing her boss's email without authorization. To the guy with the black-and-white morals. There was a high chance that her reasoning wouldn't matter, that he wouldn't listen to her plea.

But the truth was she'd grown to trust Rhys, and it was clear she wasn't getting very far on her own. Obviously it would have been better to obtain proof before involving him, but the fact of the matter was that he was *already* involved.

She'd involved him the second they slept together.

And she didn't want to lie anymore, not now that they were more than neighbors.

All she could do was hope that he was the good man she believed him to be. That he'd be able to look past her indiscretion to the bigger problem—Sean Ainslie.

"Did you know who I was when you moved into your apartment?"

"No," she said, glancing at the burger she now had no appetite for. "You being my neighbor is a coincidence."

His deep brown eyes were coldly assessing. "Did you sleep with me to make me trust you?"

A lump formed in her throat. "How could you even ask me that?"

"There's so much you haven't told me, I want to be sure."

"I'm a painter, not an actress." She pushed her fries around with a fork. "I can't fake feelings any more than I can fake orgasms."

It hadn't sounded all that dangerous in her head but the moment she'd said the words aloud her stomach pitched. Feelings. What on earth did that mean and why the hell had she clued him in?

He appeared as baffled by her admission as she was. "You do realize that you've admitted to lying to me and now you're claiming to have feelings for me?"

"It's complicated," she muttered.

"I'd say it's more than complicated."

"You know what? Maybe it isn't. *Maybe* it's incredibly simple." Frustration roiled within her, but she couldn't take it out on him. *She*'d done wrong, here. But if she could make him see it was all with good intention, he might help her. "I get that I've screwed up. I'm sorry for not being totally honest with you. I'm sorry that I let us cross a line knowing it could make things hard for your job. But I am *not* sorry that I'm here trying to get some justice for my best friend."

"What did you think was going to happen, Wren?" He rubbed at the back of his neck, a crease forming between his dark brows. "That you would come here and play spy like you're in a goddamn Hollywood movie? That you would magically find this evidence on your own and wrap everything up with a neat little bow?"

She tamped down the urge to argue with him. She *needed* him, needed to regain his trust. "Maybe."

"If Sean did assault your friend, what did you think he would do to you?" His voice was getting harder, louder. "What if he hurt you the same way? What if you weren't as lucky as your friend?"

That's when she saw it. *His* feelings…for her. He was angry and terrified. For her.

"I'm smart, Rhys. I know how to play him."

"I don't want to insult your intelligence, Wren, but what you've done is pretty damn stupid." His fists clenched. "And dangerous…and possibly illegal."

Cold fear dripped down her spine. "What happens now?"

"I don't know." His fingers dug deeper into the muscles of his neck. "But I do know you're not going near Sean Ainslie until we figure it out."

"I have to go to work. It'll tip him off if I don't. And I have to keep an eye out for Aimee."

"Why?"

"She had bruises on her arm." Wren popped a fry into her mouth and tried to force herself to eat, but it tasted like nothing. "Finger-shaped bruises. She said Sean had gotten rough with her, but when I tried to talk to her about it again today she clammed up and said she overreacted."

He shook his head, the disgust evident on his face. "Did she say what caused him to get angry?"

"Not really. She said they were arguing about a painting. He wasn't happy with what she'd done. Artistic differences, I guess."

"That doesn't seem like a reason for him to get physical."

"Do you think men who hurt women have their brains wired properly?"

He grunted. "Point taken."

"I'm convinced he's hiding something in the storage room." She gave up eating and instead pushed her food around on her plate. "That's got to be the reason he freaked out and called your company when I tried to get in. He's meticulous about making sure no one gets inside."

"How so?"

"He gave me this big spiel on my first day about how it's full of valuable paintings and that when we're setting up for a showing, only he is allowed to get the paintings out. I wasn't sure what to make of it at first—I mean, a lot of artists are eccentric and private, but he flipped out when he thought Lola was trying to get inside one day when she was mopping the floors."

"Have you ever seen him go into the room?"

"No, he must wait until we're all gone for the day. Or maybe he does it early in the morning."

"Do you think he has any paintings that are worth a lot of money?"

Wren shrugged. "I honestly don't know. I don't think he sells as many paintings as he'd like people to believe. His style is…eclectic. But not in a good way."

"What do you mean?"

"There's no common thread or general theme. A lot of artists will experiment and try new things, but in Sean's work, I can't even see an attempt to build upon a particular style or technique."

"What's he like as a teacher?"

"Pushy, talks a lot of shit that doesn't mean anything."

"What about the other girls?"

"They eat it up." Wren shook her head. "They're young and grateful that someone has given them an opportunity in an industry that's so competitive. They believe he can turn them into wunderkinds."

"That's not the case?"

"Not from what I've seen. But maybe I'm just jaded and that's affecting my view."

Wren had worked with several different art teachers over the years. They'd all given her different advice that often clashed and contradicted. Art, she'd come to realize, was like cutting out a part of your soul and showing it to the world. It hurt when people rejected what you'd made because they were, in essence, rejecting you.

And the closer you got to painting something from deep within, the more likely you were to end up bleeding.

"Why do you say you're jaded?" He looked genuinely confused.

"I'm not exactly the poster child for a successful career in the arts." She leaned back against the booth and pushed her mostly untouched plate away. "I've had more success painting faces at county fairs than I have painting on a canvas."

"You're not giving yourself enough credit."

"I am. I have to take some responsibility for what I painted and where it landed me."

She'd spent many nights wondering why she'd left the paintings in a place Christian could easily find them. Why she'd thought it a good idea to paint such provocative things in the first place. Only they weren't provocative, not really.

"How did you come to paint naked women?" Rhys asked, finally tucking into his meal.

"It happened by mistake, at first." Wren smiled at the memory. "I was planning on a series of portraits of female farmers. I put up an ad on a rural community forum saying I was looking for models and I found Cassie. When she came to my house I had a chair set up for her and she just…stripped."

"Without you asking?" A smile tugged at Rhys's full lips.

"Yep, without any warning at all. I was totally gob smacked, but I didn't know what to say…so, I painted her." Wren tentatively reached for her plate and found her appetite returning. "She had this big scar that ran up the side of her leg from a farming accident. When she tried to hide it, I asked her if she would mind me painting it. By the time we were finished she said it was the first time she'd ever felt beautiful with her scar showing. She'd never had the courage to show it to anyone and that's why she'd applied to be my model."

"To get it over with?"

"Yeah. That's when I knew what I was supposed to be painting. These women of all shapes and sizes would come to me and I would paint them as I saw them. Without their barriers or their masks or their shields. Just them and their natural beauty… Like how I painted you."

"You didn't know anything about me then," he said.

"Don't you ever meet someone and have a connection with them that defies logic? Like you see their truth." The irony of her words wasn't lost on her, but she wanted Rhys to understand how she felt. "I could tell you were a good person. I don't meet a lot of people like that."

"And I don't have the connection with anyone else that I have with you…" Silence settled over the table. Rhys looked perplexed.

"But?"

"But that doesn't mean I can ignore what you've told me tonight."

Wren wanted to reassure him that she wasn't an evil person. Sure, she seemed to make bad decision after bad decision…but it was all with good intention. That had to count for something, right?

"How long do you think Sean will keep hurting women if we don't intervene?"

"We don't have any proof he's doing that."

Her heart sank. Could he really turn a blind eye to Sean's behavior? They *didn't* have proof, sure. But Wren was certain they could find it if they worked together. At the very least they could get one of Sean's victims to speak up—and maybe if one person confessed the others would follow.

"Are you going to turn me in?" she asked.

"I need to think on it, Wren. I'm in a really difficult situation here." He seemed genuinely conflicted, and that made her feel even worse.

"But you agree that Sean is up to something, right? I know I'm not an angel, but I'm trying to figure out what's going on so he doesn't hurt anyone else." She reached for his hand across the table. His skin was warm, soft, but he didn't embrace her. Didn't give her anything back. "Please, Rhys. Give me a little more time. I'll try to get Kylie and Aimee to talk. I'm on your side."

"My side?" He pulled his hand away from her grip. "You do realize who hired me in the first place, right? My side is supposed to be *Sean's* side…which is most definitely not where you are."

"But you're investigating him, aren't you? That's why someone from your company called Kylie to ask questions. If you were just helping Sean with his security, you wouldn't be snooping around and talking to ex-employees."

"We're doing what we were hired to do, which is find out who's been trying to get access to Sean's information and why." He pulled his wallet out of his pocket and tossed a few bills onto the table. "And now I know."

"So that's it?" Wren pushed up from the table and followed him out of the diner and into the parking lot. "You don't care that he might be beating these women?"

Rhys whirled around suddenly and she almost face-planted into his chest. "That's the reason I haven't made up my mind on how I'm going to handle this yet."

So it had nothing to do with her. The realization stung, but then she'd known from the beginning that Rhys had a very strong moral code.

Shoving her pain aside, she steeled herself. "I want him to pay for what he did to my friend and I want to make sure it doesn't happen to Aimee, either. *Or* the next unsuspecting woman he hires."

"I want that, too," he said.

"Then let me help. I'll get the girls to talk, I'll keep an eye on Sean at the gallery and I can call you if anything suspicious is going on." She wrapped her arms around herself, praying that he would give her this chance. "Please."

"Fine. I'll keep this under wraps for a couple of days, but you have to promise me you won't do anything stupid."

"Don't you mean, anything *else* stupid?"

"I mean it, Wren." His features were hard; his eyes gave nothing away. "I don't want you to be the next person he hurts. I want to figure this out, but it's not worth risking your safety. You call me the *second* anything shady happens, okay?"

"I promise."

For a man who'd sworn that he wasn't protecting her, he seemed very set on making sure she kept out of harm's way.

As she stood in the parking lot of the diner, watching Rhys get into his car, she vowed that she would fix things with him. If only she could find evidence that Sean was the bad guy here, then maybe he'd forgive her for lying.

12

WREN DIALED KYLIE'S number as she walked home. It would do her good to stretch her legs before the sun went down; fresh air always seemed to create space in her mind when she felt jumbled up.

"Are you going to hang up on me again?" Kylie asked.

"I'm sorry about earlier. I had to deal with something." She rubbed at her temple while Kylie's anger simmered on the other end of the line. "And I'm sorry I've been keeping you in the dark."

"Then come home."

Wren sighed. "I can't."

"I don't understand why you're doing this."

"Because I want to help you, Ky. And this bastard shouldn't be allowed to hurt anyone else." The balmy evening breeze whispered along her bare arms. It was a beautiful night, far too serene and peaceful for her to be arguing with her best friend. "Can't you see that?"

"If you were really interested in what's best for me then you would have consulted me first instead of running off there behind my back. You're doing this for *you*."

The words were like a slap across the face. "How on earth is this for me?"

"You needed something to focus on after Christian screwed you over. You needed some kind of problem to solve, just like you *always* do when your own life isn't going according to plan." Kylie sighed. "I love you, Wren. You're the sister I never had, but don't delude yourself that this is all about helping me."

"What was I supposed to do, sit by and watch while you broke down? While he's getting away with it?"

"You could have stayed with me. You could have done what Debbie is doing. But instead, you ran away because it suited your situation."

"I wanted to help you," Wren said, swallowing the lump in her throat.

"I'm getting help...with a therapist. I'm working through what happened with a professional, Wren. You being in New York and trying to force me to talk about it *isn't* helping. It's stressing me out." Kylie's voice wavered. "Please come home."

For a moment Wren considered it. But what about Aimee? What about the next girl or the one after that?

She held her breath, debating how much to say. "There's another girl...he's hurting her, too."

The silenced seemed to stretch out for an eternity. Only the steady sound of Wren's footsteps against the pavement told her that time hadn't stopped completely. There was a faint, muffled sound on the other end of the line. Kylie was crying.

"I'm sorry, Ky." She wanted so badly to press for more details—anything that might help to gather proof against Ainslie. But her friend's tears halted her words. "I promise I'll come home as soon as I can."

"I have to go," Kylie said, her voice rough and edgy. "Maybe don't call me for a few days, okay? I need to stop thinking about this, and talking to you while you're there…"

Wren's stomach sank. "If that's what you want."

"You know what I want. I won't feel better until you're far away from him." She sniffed. "Just think about coming home. Hell, don't come home if you don't want. Go somewhere else. *Anywhere* else."

"I'll call you next week."

"Why don't I call you…when I'm ready."

Wren blinked back the first prickle of tears. "Okay."

She ended the call and brushed the back of her hand against a tear that had dropped onto her cheek as she walked up the path to her building. The sky had turned dark and the temperature had dropped. Goose bumps rippled across her skin.

How was it possible that she'd screwed up so badly while having the best intentions? Rhys was angry at her. Kylie was angry at her. Debbie…well, her sister wasn't angry but she resented Wren leaving her behind.

Wren trudged up the stairs of the walk-up, her mind swirling like a tornado. She tried to shake off the bad feeling that had settled into her bones. Rhys was right; what she'd done was stupid and naive. She hadn't helped Kylie; in fact, she seemed to have made things worse.

But Aimee still needs your help. She's still in danger. If you don't stand up to Sean, who knows what might happen to her?

As she walked to her front door, her gaze snagged on Rhys's apartment. She was tempted to knock, but it was probably best to give him time to cool down. After all, she'd dropped a pretty big bombshell on him tonight.

Wren walked into her apartment and had been inside for all of five minutes when a knock on the door made her heart leap into her throat. Had Rhys decided to come to her? The thought filled her with warmth.

She rushed to the door and opened it, the smile dying on her lips when she saw that her visitor wasn't Rhys. It was Sean.

"I hope you don't mind me showing up on your doorstep," he said, sounding decidedly uncaring. "I want to clear up this tension between us."

Wren swallowed down her instinct to slam the door in his face. "What do you mean?"

"You're not being honest with me. A true artist doesn't bottle his or her feelings up, Wren. That's why you're having issues with your paintings. You're suppressed." He swayed and planted a hand on the door frame, leaning in. "You have no idea how to tap into your true self."

The scent of stale whiskey invaded her nostrils. "Have you been drinking?"

"So what if I have?" He stepped forward and pushed her back into her apartment, slamming the door shut behind him. "Are you judging me? I should have known after I hired that twit Kylie that everyone from your hick fucking town was a purist prude."

"I told you, Kylie and I have nothing to do with one another," she lied, warning bells ringing in her ears. "And I still don't understand why you're here."

"'I still don't understand why you're here,'" he mimicked in a high-pitched voice. "Who's the boss, Wren?"

"You are." She forced herself to breathe slow and even.

"Are you sure you believe that? Because I'm getting a strong vibe of insubordination from you." He raked a hand through his long, dark hair and a chunky gold ring glinted on his right hand. It looked like the kind of ring that could do a hell of a lot of damage if it connected to bone.

Like shattering an eye socket, perhaps?

"I want…I want what's best for our working relationship," she stammered. "I value my position at the studio and if I've done something—"

"Bullshit," he spat. "You know *exactly* what you've done."

Her mind spun. Was he referring to her getting into his email? Setting off the alarm on the storage room? Had he discovered the truth about her and Kylie?

"Spare me the deer-in-headlights look, Wren." He rolled his eyes. "I know you've been talking to Aimee about me."

Damn. "I just wanted to make sure she was okay."

"It's none of your business." His voice escalated, taking on the shrill edge of a person about to lose their shit. "You ought to be careful, being so nosy. I might think you were the one trying to hack into my account and delete my emails if you weren't so stupid and obvious."

Wren said a silent thank-you for small mercies. For as long as Sean didn't suspect her, she could talk her way out of her supposed indiscretion.

"You're right," she said, hanging her head. "I shouldn't have talked to her about it."

For a moment she thought she'd appeased him. He glanced around her apartment as if he'd forgotten why he was there. But then his eyes landed on something behind her and a dark shadow rolled across his face.

"What is *that*?" he thundered.

"What?" Wren whirled around and cursed under her breath when she saw what he was looking at.

The portrait of Rhys.

"Why are you painting someone from the security company?"

"I don't know what you're talking about," she said quickly, but the words were breathless and hurried. "It's just a man."

She was about to turn when pain burned at her scalp. Sean fisted his hands in her hair and dragged her toward the painting.

"Explain yourself," he said into her ear. The words were a mere whisper, and yet it frightened her more than if he'd yelled. "Tell me why the fuck you have a painting of Rhys Glover in your apartment."

RHYS STOPPED HIS car at a red light. He'd driven block after block, hoping that the answer to his problems might be around the next corner. But a good half an hour after he'd left Wren at the diner, he was still at a loss.

Why the hell hadn't he seen this coming?

Anger at himself roiled with frustration at Wren. She was so...idealistic. And impulsive.

And spontaneous and sexy and so damn beautiful.

"You're a glutton for punishment," he muttered to his reflection in the rearview mirror.

He drove home deep in thought. But no matter how hard he tried, the solution wouldn't come. There wasn't a magic bullet. No matter which way he turned he was doing wrong by someone.

Pissed as he was that she'd lied to him, he understood her reasons and admired her fierce loyalty to her friend. What he would have given to have someone stick up for him like that when he was growing up...

Still, Logan would flip if he found out that Rhys had

gotten involved with a suspect. While security consultants might not be held to the same standard as police officers or other law agents, his boss *was* ex-military. And he ran a tight ship.

Rhys parked his car and headed up to his apartment. Maybe he should cut things off at the pass by telling Wren he couldn't see her again. It would draw a line between them, a line not to be crossed until this thing with Sean Ainslie was over.

But then what? The *only* reason she was in New York was to snoop around the gallery. Once that was tied up she'd be headed back home. He pounded his feet into the stairs as if it might expel the frustration from his body.

It wasn't worth risking his job for something temporary, no matter how much he enjoyed her company, both in *and* out of the bedroom. Perhaps it made him a boring rule-follower, but that's how he wanted to live his life. It's how he'd *always* lived his life.

And when has following the rules gotten you what you want?

Shaking off the doubt, he climbed the last few stairs to their shared floor. Cooling things off with Wren was necessary right now. At least until he had a plan for the Ainslie Ave assignment.

Rhys crossed the narrow hallway to her front door and lifted his hand to knock. Raised voices halted him and he pressed his ear to the door. It was hard to make out specific words but he could detect a man's voice, deep and forceful. A second later there was a whimpering sound and then silence.

It might be nothing. But given Wren's involvement with a man suspected of beating women, he couldn't risk ignoring his instincts. He strained to hear through the door, but everything had gone quiet.

"Shit," he muttered under his breath.

A muffled sob broke the silence, and the sound speared through Rhys's heart. Wren wasn't the kind of person to cry at anything small, but he also didn't want to bust into her apartment and interrupt something personal.

He hesitated until he heard something that sounded like "please, stop." The arguing started up again, but Wren's voice was drowned out by the deep timbre of a man.

A man who sounded a lot like Sean Ainslie.

Shit.

Rhys tested the handle, knowing that the doors didn't automatically lock when they closed. He hoped Wren's landlord hadn't installed any additional security like he had.

The handle eased down and he let out a small sigh of relief. Now all he had to do was get himself into the room and convince Sean to back down. This was well out of the realm of his training at Cobalt & Dane—he was the guy who could crack firewalls and follow a digital trail. He didn't rescue people.

The door opened soundlessly and he saw that Sean had a fistful of Wren's hair. They were facing a painting, *his* painting.

"Please," Wren pleaded. "You're hurting me."

"You need to come clean," Sean growled. "Don't make me force it out of you."

"Sean Ainslie," Rhys thundered. "You let her go right fucking now."

"Let me guess, it must be her partner in crime." Sean turned around, Wren's hair still in his fist.

"We know what you've been doing," Rhys said, stepping forward. His whole body was charged with furious energy.

Rhys wasn't a violent guy by any means—he'd always described himself as a lover, not a fighter. But all Sean could see was that Rhys had a good half a foot and at least twenty-five pounds over him. Not to mention the sight of him hurting Wren was enough to make Rhys want to Hulk smash Ainslie's face.

"You don't know shit and neither does she."

Wren's blue eyes were wide and she winced as he jerked her head. "Let me go."

"In fact," Sean continued, "I'll wager that your boss will be pretty pissed to hear that you're involved with your client's employee. That's poor form, Rhys. You're fucking her, aren't you?"

"If you don't let her go, I'll make it so that you can't use that hand ever again." He sucked in a breath, his fists shaking at his sides. "And then I'm going to make sure she presses charges for assault. I'm confident there are other women who would have a similar story to share."

Tension vibrated in the air as Sean stayed silent, his grip tight at Wren's scalp. Her head was bent to lessen the strain, but the redness around her eyes and blotchiness on her cheeks told him all he needed to know. He was going to nail Sean Ainslie to the wall. But he'd do it *his* way…by the book.

"Fine." Sean released Wren and she gasped in relief as she stumbled backward, her hands going to her head. Sean walked right up to Rhys, cocky as ever, and tapped him on the chest. "I'll still be putting a call into your boss. It's Logan, isn't it? I've met him before. Nice guy,

I'm sure he'll be keen to hear about his company's dead-weight."

"Rhys." Wren's voice was low and warning. "Let him leave."

But he couldn't let Sean go, not that easily. He thumped a hand down on the other man's shoulder and leaned in. "There's a special place in hell for men who hurt women. I will personally ensure that you end up there."

Sean laughed and knocked Rhys's hand away. "We'll see. You remember that my father is a judge, right?"

"*Was* a judge," Rhys said through gritted teeth.

"Still got the connections." Sean winked and left them alone in the apartment.

"Don't you dare go after him," Wren said, wrapping her arms around herself. Her slender frame started to shake. "I don't want you doing anything that might come back to hurt you. Although it sounds like you already have."

"It'll be fine."

"Will it?" She went to the front door and turned the lock. "He said he was going to call your boss."

"He doesn't have proof of anything."

But Rhys had no idea how Logan would take it *or* if he would believe Sean. Either way, there would be some explaining to do. Clients didn't usually accuse the consultants of sleeping with their staff and compromising an investigation.

"I'm so sorry I've dragged you into this," she said, her brows furrowed.

"This is my job. I was already involved." He closed the distance between them and reached out to touch her face. "I heard shouting coming from your apartment and…"

"Thank you," she whispered. "He showed up and bullied his way in. He was angry that I'd been talking to Aimee about him—"

"Shit, Wren." He squeezed his eyes shut. "This isn't a game. I don't want to imagine what might have happened if I hadn't been on my way over. He could've really hurt you."

"I know, I know. But he mentioned something about deleted emails. Can Quinn find it? I know Aimee deleted something from his email account, but there might also be proof that he's got something shady going on."

"We have proof. He came here tonight to threaten you."

"And what am I going to tell the police? That he pulled my hair?"

"It's assault, Wren."

"What he did to the other girls was assault." She sighed and pulled his hand to her cheek. "Maybe we can get Aimee and Kylie to press charges, and the other girls, too—"

"You need to let it go, let Cobalt & Dane handle it. I don't want you going back to the gallery." Rhys sighed. "Though after he calls Logan we will probably no longer be employed by Ainslie Ave."

"But you've got access to the security cameras, right?"

"Not if he terminates his contract with us." He held up his hand when Wren opened her mouth to argue. "But that's a problem for tomorrow."

Right now, he wanted to wrap himself up in her. The fear he'd experienced tonight had worn him down. His mind whirred with the what-ifs—what if he hadn't heard the commotion from her apartment? What if he hadn't decided to go to her in the first place? What if Logan fired him and then she left, anyway?

"You look so upset," she said softly.

"I'm not upset. I'm relieved you're safe, I'm worried about tomorrow and I'm frustrated at myself for handling things badly." He pulled her toward him. "But things are what they are—nothing we can do to change the past."

"You're right." She nodded, pressing her cheek against his chest.

He wrapped his arms around her small shoulders and let himself hold her tight. He allowed his body to enjoy the way she fitted against him, let her touch feed the gnawing ache inside him. No matter how he tried to erase his desire with logic and rules, he felt good with her. He felt…satisfied.

That didn't happen often, if ever. His life was a constant climb, chasing one thing after another. Trying to be better. Trying to be more. Trying to be worthy. But with her, all that restlessness fell away.

"Do you want something to eat?" she asked, tilting her face up to his. "Maybe some dessert?"

"Dessert is the last thing on my mind, Wren."

"Then what is on your mind?"

Tomorrow was going to be a shit show. When Sean called Logan, he could lose his job. At the very least he'd be in Logan's bad books, and that was not a place anyone wanted to be.

Screw it. He'd already fucked things up royally; he may as well enjoy tonight before it all came crashing down.

"You," he said, leaning down to brush his lips against hers. "Just you."

13

WREN SIGHED AS he peppered kisses along her jaw. His breath was heavier now, his muscular arms tightening around her. Only they didn't feel restricting, they felt like her safe place. They felt like protection. Instinct took over and she leaned forward, her tongue brushing the skin on his neck. When she drew back and looked up at him, her heart was in her mouth.

The buckle of his belt and the hard length of his erection dug into her belly. His mouth found hers, hot and desperate and open. His hands thrust up into her hair and he tilted her head back, kissing her deeply. Entirely. The world tilted around them.

"I want you, Wren, and I can't seem to stop wanting you."

He was torn; she could hear it in his voice. He was a good man, a principled man, and she'd come along and dragged him into her craziness. But she couldn't stay away from him, either. "Please," she breathed. "Don't stop."

Suddenly her back was against the wall, though she'd scarcely been aware of moving. He hoisted her skirt up, bunching the fabric at her waist with one hand, and wrenched her leg over his hip. The fly of his pants rubbed at her aching sex. She wished she'd gone commando; there was too much of a barrier between them.

His mouth was at her neck, lips sucking and tongue flicking and teeth scraping. He kissed along her jaw and found her mouth again. The faint stubble on his face lightly scratched her cheek and she knew tomorrow there would be subtle marks all over her. Marks that would make her body burn with the memory of tonight.

His hand found the hem of her top and slipped underneath it, palming her breast so slowly she thought she might explode with desperation. She reached for his belt buckle and struggled to loosen it.

"Is this a security belt?" she panted, gasping as his deft fingers found her nipple through the thin lace of her bra. Mercifully, his belt gave way.

His throaty laugh rolled over her skin, sending a shiver down her spine. "Got to protect the goods."

"You're always so cautious," she teased. "So careful."

"I don't want to be careful now." He paused his assault on her senses and rested his forehead against her. Her hand stilled at his waist.

"Why?"

His eyes were endless and deep, the warm brown gaze almost turning her to liquid on the spot. That stare could do a lot of damage; it could make her trust again. Make her feel like maybe it was okay to be her crazy, impulsive self.

"Because I know this is wrong. I should be trying to think about how I'm going to save my job…" His hands cupped her face, the pads of his thumbs brushing her cheekbones. "But I don't care."

"You should care." She closed her eyes. "Your job is important."

"Yes, it is. But nothing I do tonight will change the course of what's going to happen." His lips pressed to hers. "And right now all I want is to hold you and be as deep inside you as I can."

The words made her whole body tense in anticipation. "I want that, too."

Without warning, he picked her up and carried her to her bedroom. She locked her mouth over his, the force of her kiss almost bringing them both to the ground as they walked into the dark room. Her hand groped for the light, but he was moving too fast.

"You really need a bed frame," he groaned as he knelt down, still cradling her in his arms. She felt his muscles flex as he moved, the sheer strength of him stoking the fire inside her.

"At least mattresses don't squeak."

As he laid her down, their legs tangled. Without light all she could do was feel. Already her hands seemed to know his body, seemed to understand how to touch him.

She found the bulge of his cock trapped behind wool trousers and she cupped him. Even with the barrier, heat radiated from him. She used her other hand to bring his head down to hers. The easy slide of his tongue between her lips was almost enough to make her come on the spot.

Her fingers found his zipper and she drew it down, her mind focused on nothing but getting the hard length of him in her greedy grasp. Twisting so she could get her hands down the front of his boxer briefs, she drew him out.

"That's what I want," she whispered. He was hard as rock, pulsing and sensitive.

He swore under his breath as she thumbed the head of him, spreading a drop of precum around.

"Christ," he hissed. "You'd better slow that down."

She squeezed. "Or what?"

His lips were at her ear, his breath hot on her skin. "Or I'll have to flip you over right now and make sure I at least get inside you before I come."

An involuntary whimper escaped her. "That sounds pretty good to me."

Her eyes were slowly adjusting to the dark, and the outline of him had formed against the city lights filtering in through her blinds. The streetlights winked. Between the darkness and the reassuring weight of him pressing her into the mattress, she didn't want to move. Ever.

This was it, she realized. This was what it was like to feel loved. To feel protected and cherished. To feel wanted.

Even after all she'd done, he'd been there when she needed him.

Her chest clenched as the thought replayed over and over in her head, like a needle catching on a scratched record.

She resisted the idea—this wasn't love. It was lust, mutual attraction. Affection, perhaps, but not love.

You get that out of your head right now.

Refocusing, she worked her hand up and down Rhys's cock. His moans urged her on. The way he thrust his hips forward to meet her momentum should be enough for her. His body should be enough.

He's a great guy, but he only did what he felt was right. It's about his morals, not about you.

Then why did she want more from him?

"Stop it," he growled and she jumped, her mind automatically connecting his words with her thoughts before she realized that he couldn't know what she was thinking. "You're too damn good at that."

He brushed her hand aside and crawled down her body. His hands were on her legs, shoving the fabric of her skirt up her thighs, his lips blazing a trail from her knee to her hip. Not a second was wasted; this wasn't about teasing or about drawing out the inevitable.

He was impatient and she loved it.

"You need to stop wearing panties," he said as he yanked at the waistband of her underwear.

"Yes, sir." She lifted her hips and he undressed her roughly, without finesse.

But then his mouth pressed against her sex and all the tension in her body evaporated. His full lips worked her like he'd studied her for years. As if he knew the exact pressure, the exact speed with which to propel her into nirvana.

"God, Rhys." She reached for his head.

The steady flick of his tongue over her clit was maddening. A tremor started in her thighs as she fought to hang on, fought to make it last more than a few seconds. But he was too good for that, and soon she was flying over the edge, her hips rocking against his face while she took everything he offered her.

He had crawled up beside her before she'd even realized that he'd moved. "I love the sound you make when I'm between your legs."

"I make a sound?" She honestly could have been doing the Macarena for all she knew. When he touched her, her mind became a blank slate.

"It's like a kitten trying to growl." He was already undressing her, tugging her tank top over her head. "Sexy *and* sweet."

"I'm glad you enjoy it."

"I could listen to that sound all day."

She pushed her skirt down and wriggled until she was able to kick it off into the dark room. "I wish I could let you be down there all day, but I don't think my body could handle it."

"I'm game if you are." The sound of fabric rustling cut through the quiet, and soon he was naked and on top of her.

The hairs on his legs brushed her sensitive skin as he nudged his thigh between hers. Her teeth clamped down onto her lower lip as he guided her hand back to him.

"Oh, so *now* you want it," she teased, relishing the weight of him in her palm.

"I want it like nothing else." He shifted, easing her legs apart. "I want you wrapped around me, Wren. I want to feel how tight you are."

She fumbled around for the condoms she'd finally remembered to pick up from the store. Her fingers brushed the foil packets and she handed one over to him. The sound of foil tearing sent pleasure rushing through her like a drug.

It made everything slow down and speed up at the same time. Lolling her head against the mattress, she waited as he sheathed himself. It was sweet torture. A second later, the fat head of his cock pressed at her entrance. They hovered there, feeding off each other's anticipation. Then he plunged into her.

As he moved inside her, she wrapped her legs around

him and clung to him. His face pressed against her neck and she cupped his head, holding him to her as though it were the end.

It most likely was. In the morning he would realize he'd made a mistake, and soon she would be going home. Blinking back tears, she pressed her lips to his cheek, urging him on with soft whispers.

With a final thrust, his whole body shook. There was no air between them; there was nothing that would force them apart. Except tomorrow.

RHYS PACED UP and down in front of Logan's office. He hadn't even made it into the Cobalt & Dane headquarters before he'd been summoned with a terse email. This was it. All his hard work fighting to get people to believe in him, to believe in his talents, would be over.

Never before had he felt so conflicted. He was angry— at himself rather than at Wren. How could he have not suspected her? Was a pretty face all it took to throw him off his game?

But that was the problem, Wren wasn't just a pretty face, and that was *exactly* why he'd wanted to get close to her. She was inspiring, refreshing. She made his blood pump harder. Her spontaneity called to him, which was odd. It should have bothered him how she never planned anything or how she never spent time worrying about sensible things like buying a bed frame or throwing her underwear into a clothes hamper. She probably didn't even own a clothes hamper.

It certainly bothered him that she'd put herself into a potentially dangerous situation for something that wasn't her problem.

Yet he was breaking the rules for her. Something that went totally against his nature.

It's because you know she's right. Sean Ainslie has proved what he'll do to get his own way, and you have a responsibility to make sure you listen to the facts.

But the fact was, Wren had done the wrong thing by trying to dig into Sean's business. Still, he could rationalize his decision to keep quiet because she hadn't stolen anything and her attempt to access Sean's storage room had failed. Therefore, her indiscretions were minor. He just had to make sure they stayed that way.

You'd better hope to hell she took your advice to steer clear of the gallery.

He shook his head. If he'd been able to take the day off to make sure she didn't leave her apartment, he would have.

He pushed down the worry and tried to prepare himself for the beat down he was about to get. For a brief second he'd toyed with the idea of lying, but he'd dismissed it just as quickly. Tough but fair, that was his motto. And he hadn't gotten that way by being dishonest.

"He'll see you now," Logan's assistant said.

Rhys pushed open the door and walked in with his head held high. Sure, he'd made a mistake but he was still the same person, still the same guy who prided himself on following the rules and doing the right thing.

"What the fuck went down last night?" Logan raked a hand through his longish hair. "Sean Ainslie called me at the ass crack of dawn to say that you physically threatened him."

"Did he tell you that I threatened him *after* he attacked one of his staff members?" Rhys braced his hands on the back of a chair facing Logan's desk.

The room was bright and airy, thanks to a window that overlooked Manhattan. Yet no amount of sunlight could make this room feel warm and inviting. Logan had an air of authority that chilled even the warmest space.

"He said that he'd gone to meet one of his employees to talk about a work issue and that you barged into her apartment and threatened to break his hands." Logan shook his head. "For starters, what were you doing at her apartment after-hours?"

"She lives in the same building as I do—her apartment is the one across the hall from mine. I heard yelling."

"So you know this woman...?" He looked down at his notes. "Wren Livingston."

"She was new to my building. We'd met a few times in passing before we started investigating Ainslie's complaint." He left out the bit where she'd showed him her erotic paintings. "But I didn't know she worked for Ainslie until the day that Quinn and I went to the gallery."

"Did you make a note of it in your report?"

"No."

His brows furrowed. "Why not?"

"I didn't think she was involved."

"You mean to tell me that you immediately ruled out the employee of a client with a security breach even though the signs pointed to it being an inside job?" Logan rubbed a hand over his face and exhaled. "Why would you do that?"

"She didn't appear to have any motive."

"And you determined that how?"

This was where things got messy, because he'd determined it based on gut instinct, which wouldn't fly with Logan. Hell, if one of Rhys's employees had come to him with the same story, it wouldn't have flown with him, either.

"She didn't appear to have the skills to break into Ainslie's account."

"Because lurking in someone else's email requires a lot of technical skill, does it?" Logan held up a hand. "That's bullshit and you know it. I want you to be straight with me, Glover. Because I can tell something is going on here and I will *not* be kept in the dark."

Rhys drew in a long, deep breath. "Quinn and I came across information that indicated Sean Ainslie was assaulting his employees. Wren Livingston was able to corroborate this information for us, and then, last night, I saw it for myself. He came to her apartment and physically assaulted her. If I hadn't overheard them fighting, she'd be in much worse shape than she is currently."

"How did evidence of assault come up in the course of a routine security monitoring job?" Logan dropped down into his seat, his expression guarded but his tone no longer filled with ice.

Rhys ran Logan through everything they'd found— from the digging Quinn had done into Ainslie's ex-employees to the conversations between Wren and Aimee.

"But," Rhys continued, "what tipped us off first was that he had a monitored security service for the building and some heavy-duty protection on his storage room, but no cameras."

"According to his file, we installed the alarm system for the building about eight years ago." Logan leaned forward and looked at his laptop screen. "The security room was done five years ago. Since then we've only had the odd incident response call and two site visits for equipment maintenance. Nothing in here about security cameras."

"Don't you think it's odd to go to all that trouble with the outside of the building and for one room, but not to put cameras inside the place?"

"That is unusual," Logan said with a slow nod of his head. "But it's not our job to investigate our clients. They hire us for a purpose and we fulfill that purpose. This is a service job, Rhys. We're not the FBI."

"Is Ainslie still a client?"

Logan sighed. "I told him to take a few days to calm down and that I'd talk to you about what happened last night. In the meantime, I have promised him that you won't be going anywhere near him *or* Ainslie Ave."

"So you don't think we should intervene if people are being hurt?"

"I didn't say that." He motioned for Rhys to take a seat. That was Logan's way of saying that he was willing to listen. "But I need you to be honest with me. Are you emotionally invested in this girl?"

The question came out of nowhere. Rhys had been prepared to be asked if he was sleeping with Wren, if he felt she'd used sex to manipulate him. If he understood that getting physical with the employee of a client was wrong.

But not this.

"Answer the question, Glover."

It had started out physical. It was *still* physical. But last night had taken things to a whole new level, an emotional level. He'd slept with his arms around her, fearful that something might happen if he let her go. Even if that meant spending the night on her shitty mattress on the ground and waking up feeling like his spine had been turned into a pretzel.

It wasn't just that he was worried for her safety… He didn't want her to go home to Idaho. Realization ebbed through him like a drug. This wasn't just about seeing where things might go. He *knew* where they would go; he knew they would work together.

They would be happy.

"Yes," he said, the word making him feel relieved and yet more burdened. "I'm emotionally invested."

"Wrong answer." Logan stretched his neck from side to side. "If we're potentially going to breach our service contract, I want to be damn sure we're doing it for the right reason. And your heart is *not* the right reason."

"Is that your way of saying you believe me about Ainslie?"

"I do. He's always seemed like a cagey son of a bitch, but no one ever put two and two together before you and your team." He drummed his fingers against the desktop, his expression still unreadable. Logan had a hell of a poker face. "But that doesn't mean I'm stupid enough to keep you on this assignment. You'll hand it over to Owen and he'll run with it from now on. Quinn can support him and you can observe, but that's it."

Okay, so at least he wasn't getting fired.

"What about Wren?" He knew it looked bad to even ask, but there was no way in hell he was letting anything happen to her. Pride be damned.

"We'll keep eyes on Ainslie while this all goes down."

"Thank you."

"You're not off the hook, Rhys. Be thankful you still have a job, but I'll expect you to work your ass off to get back in my good books."

A few weeks ago those words would have ended him. But now, knowing that he was doing something for a higher purpose than just furthering himself and his career, he could take it. For Wren, he could endure a lot worse.

14

WREN SAT IN a meeting room at the front of the Cobalt & Dane offices, staring at a wall clock. Each time the second hand moved, it made a ticking sound that was starting to drive her insane. She didn't need a reminder that the minutes were slowly melting away.

Rhys had left her apartment in the wee hours of the morning, claiming he needed to be at work as early as possible. After he'd left, she'd tossed and turned, unable to sleep for worrying about how badly she'd messed up his life.

"Wren, thanks for coming down," Quinn said as she walked into the room, with Rhys in tow. "Sorry to drag you in here without much notice."

Relief eased through her chest. At least he hadn't been fired. "It's fine."

Rhys nodded at her but didn't say anything. The line between his eyes told her he'd had a rough morning.

"So Rhys has updated me on what's been going on with Sean, including that he came to your apartment last night. Is that correct?"

Quinn made notes as Wren relayed what'd happened,

leaving out the part about Rhys staying over...just in case that information wasn't widely known.

"We're going to monitor the gallery through the security cameras that we've set up." Quinn tapped her pen against the edge of the table. "Now, if you have any contact with either Lola or Aimee, please don't mention this. We don't want to spook Sean."

"Of course."

"We're breaking our contract with him by doing this," Rhys said. "So it's really important that we keep this activity quiet."

A lump formed in her throat. "I understand. I promise I won't say anything."

"We'll monitor the cameras for a couple of days and see if Sean accesses the storage room. I understand you think he's hiding something in there?" Quinn said, watching her with hawk-like eyes.

"That's right, but I have no idea what."

"I didn't see anything but paintings when I was in there. I made sure to look thoroughly, too, because I suspected the same thing," she said. "It was literally just dozens of paintings. Some very strange ones, too."

"Oh?" Wren tried to listen to Quinn while pretending that she wasn't slowly driving herself crazy trying to figure out what Rhys was thinking.

"Yeah, some weird paintings with vegetables that had faces," Quinn said with a shake of her head.

"Like an angry carrot with a pitchfork?" Wren asked, her blood suddenly running cold.

"Yeah." Quinn glanced up sharply.

"And a screaming pumpkin?" She knew the painting exactly—right down to the brushes that had created the strange and haunting image.

"Yes."

"They're meant to represent the plight of farmers in today's society and the issues around agricultural decline," she said, echoing the words she'd heard once before, when the idea of the collection had been conceived.

"Are you very familiar with all of Sean's paintings?"

"He didn't paint them. My friend Kylie did."

The pieces of the puzzle started to fall into place. Why Sean was so secretive about the storage room. Why Kylie had refused to let Wren come into her studio after she'd returned from New York. Why the Ainslie Ave shows seemed to be weirdly eclectic and lacking in direction.

Because none of them were Sean's paintings.

"Why would he have her paintings if she's no longer working at the gallery? Would she have sold them to him?" Quinn asked.

"He's stealing them," she said, her heartbeat kicking up a notch. "I saw him carrying a painting the other day that seemed familiar, but I couldn't place it at the time. I remember now. It looked a lot like one that Aimee was finishing up when I first started at the gallery."

"Can you prove it?" Rhys asked, his hands bunching into fists on top of the table.

"I'm sure I have a picture of Kylie while she was painting the pumpkin. She'd started working on it before she left for New York, and I told her I wanted a picture before she got famous." The image was clear in her mind—her friend standing at the canvas, wearing her pink apron as she always did when she painted. The idea was fresh, weird. She had been sure it would get her noticed in the art world.

It had. But she'd been noticed by the wrong person.

"I did think it was strange how Sean seemed to only

hire young women from small towns," Wren added. "None of us have the fancy education that most galleries require for our work. Kylie thought that meant he was looking for pure talent. The kind of rawness and honesty that some of those rich students don't have. But what he really wanted were girls who were desperate and far away from home."

How stupid had she been to come here? How stupid had she been not to stop Kylie from coming?

"I guess he figures it's a low-risk scam since none of the gallery's customers are likely to recognize the paintings of an unknown artist. And if he traumatizes the true artists, they're too scared and ashamed to say anything. But he takes the precaution of hiding the paintings in this locked room in case one of the interns happens to recognize the paintings…as I did. I told him that Kylie and I were no longer friends because I didn't want him to suspect my reason for accepting the internship, but I guess he was worried I'd see one of her paintings there."

"If we can get footage from the storage room of her paintings, that might be enough to charge him with theft," Quinn said, her face intensely serious.

Rhys shook his head. "His father was a judge. We need something concrete or else it won't stick."

Rhys was right; his father would no doubt do everything in his power to get Sean off the hook. They needed an admission from Sean on *why* he'd done what he'd done. Something he couldn't wriggle away from.

The reason she'd never seen him working on a painting himself was because he had no talent. So he stole it from others, hoping to find his golden goose.

An idea sprang to Wren's mind.

"I'll get him to confess," she said.

Rhys shook his head vehemently. "You're not going anywhere near Sean Ainslie."

"Hear me out." She held up a hand. "You can put a wire on me or give me a recording advice. I'll confront him at the gallery and get him to say that he's been stealing the paintings and abusing these women."

"No fucking way."

"Hang on," Quinn interjected. "Shouldn't we at least run this past Owen? It might be our best bet at making sure we nail this guy once and for all."

Rhys looked as though he were about to explode. She hadn't ever seen him so furious, not even last night when he'd confronted Sean. Normally he was cool, calm and collected. Ever the guy in control of his environment. But now a muscle in his jaw twitched, and his arms were folded tightly across his chest.

"Can you give us a minute?" he said to Quinn.

"Sure thing." She got up and left the room, closing the glass door with a soft click.

Neither one of them said anything at first, and Wren had to stop herself from wrenching the clock off the wall and stomping on it until that damn ticking stopped.

"You're not going in there," he said, his voice brittle. "It's too risky."

"What happens if I don't? He'll get away with it. Then he'll find another girl and do the same thing all over again. It's not right."

"I won't risk your safety for this, Wren. No way in hell."

"You're not the one risking my safety. *I* am. It's my decision to make, not yours."

"You're so...impulsive." He threw his hands up in the air. "Have you thought this through at all? What if he attacks you like he did last night? What if something goes wrong?"

"I understand there are risks, but I'm willing to take them." She drew a steadying breath. "I want to help."

He rubbed his hands over his face, his dark brows knitted together. "Think about yourself for once, Wren. Put *yourself* first. You don't have to always be looking out for other people."

"What else am I going to do?"

Since she'd come to New York, her life had been a crazy ride. But she'd felt so…free. Being with Rhys had allowed her to be comfortable in her skin, to enjoy sex, to not be ashamed of what she wanted to paint. Not only that, she'd finally been able to pick up her brushes again without being paralyzed by fear. She'd painted again because of him.

But Sean Ainslie's crimes would hang over her head unless she made sure he got his due.

"Maybe do what most people do. Get a job, find something you're passionate about…some*one* you're passionate about."

"Maybe I'm not like most people."

Part of her wanted to buy into the fantasy that she could stay in New York. Stay with Rhys. But that wasn't going to happen.

She owed it to Kylie to finally be a good friend by doing something that would actually help her heal. What she should have done in the first place—be there for her. In person.

Her friend had been right. Wren had run away because it suited her, because she'd wanted distance from her own problems. But now she knew that she had the strength to stand up to the bullies and the liars. If she stood up to

Sean and helped to put him away, then she could face the people of Charity Springs. She could return home to the people that needed her, like Kylie and Debbie.

She could be the person who'd done something good, for once.

"Then what are you going to do after this is all done?" he asked.

"I'm going home."

THE WORDS CUT right into him. Silly him, assuming she'd consider staying in New York.

Staying with *him*.

After last night he thought things might be different between them. He'd shown her that he believed her, that he listened to her. Cared about her. But apparently that didn't count for anything.

"You're going back there?" He ran a hand over his head, trying to tamp down the anger that was rearing up within him. "To that hick town where the people call you a sexual deviant?"

"It's my home, Rhys." She blinked at him, her brows furrowed. "I never said I was planning to make a life here."

"You ran away from that place because of how they treated you, and all of a sudden you're feeling the pull of loyalty." He shook his head. "I thought you hated that place."

"I'm angry about what happened to me, of course, but my family is there. Kylie is there… She needs me."

"What do *you* need, Wren?" He stood, shoving back his chair so hard it almost toppled over. "Because it's hard for me to tell whether or not you care about your future. You seem to base all of your actions on other people."

"No, I don't." Her face reddened in a way that told him she knew damn well he was right.

"No? You came here to find justice for your friend. You're now offering to put yourself at risk to get Sean Ainslie to confess." He ticked the items off his fingers. "And let's not forget how you buttered me up to make sure I wouldn't turn you in."

"That is *not* true." Her face looked as though it might crumple, but instead she stood and drew in a deep breath.

"Isn't it? Because from my standpoint, it seems like everything you've done is to serve someone else. You don't live your own life."

"I do. I spent time with you because I *cared* about you."

Cared. Past tense.

Because now she didn't need anything from him. The realization that she'd used him was like a slap across the face.

"You don't get to say that to me." The frustration tumbled out of him unbidden. "Not after you've screwed my reputation only to throw it back in my face by putting yourself in danger."

The hurt that streaked across her face wrenched like a knife in his chest. "I didn't force you to sleep with me."

"My record here has been one hundred percent clean. I have been a model employee until this. And now my reputation is on the line, and for what?"

She'd let him believe she wasn't involved when she was and, worse than that, she'd let him believe that he meant something to her. That he was important and real and visible.

"I'm sorry, okay?" She threw her hands up in the air. "It was selfish, I know that. But I wanted to help my friend and…I liked you. You were the first guy who's ever made me feel like I'm not useless and wrong. If I could change things, I would."

"Well, you can't. I'll have to earn back Logan's trust, and he's not the kind of guy who dishes it out easily."

"What do you want me to say?" she said, wrapping her arms around herself.

I want you to tell me I mean something to you.

"If you don't know what I want from you, then it's clear you don't actually care for me at all."

She looked so small and vulnerable, and his instincts urged him to bundle her up in his arms. But he couldn't touch her again, not now that he knew how little he'd meant to her. The thought of staying with him hadn't even crossed her mind.

"Are you trying to hurt my feelings?" she asked, her voice coated in frustration.

"This isn't about feelings. It's about actions."

She shook her head and sucked on her cheek, though he could still see the tremble in her lip. "Have you ever thought that maybe life isn't all black-and-white? You can't just spreadsheet everything out and use a formula to make a decision."

"Do you think that's what I did last night?" Damn it, she had a way of dragging him out of his logical mindset into dangerous emotional territory. "Do you think I came to your apartment because a formula told me so?"

She blinked. "Well—"

"No, I came to your apartment because I couldn't stand the idea of not clearing the air between us. When I saw Sean there…" Why was he even bothering? "You know what? It doesn't matter. You've made up your mind."

"I never meant to hurt you."

"Just promise me one thing," he said. "At some point in your life, you'll start basing your decisions on what *you* want instead of hiding behind everyone else's needs."

15

WREN FELT AS if the air had been sucked from her lungs. He made her sound so...weak.

But the truth was, she couldn't stay in New York. She had no job, no purpose. When she wasn't on a mission for someone else she had no direction. What was she supposed to do? Sit around all day working on paintings that would never sell while slowly dying from the fear that Rhys would one day realize she was talentless? That she wasn't going anywhere in life?

He was a go-getter. A person totally in control of his life, of his career. He would be successful in whatever he chose to do.

"Is it so bad that I want to do right by the people in my life?" She asked, hoisting her bag over one shoulder. "That I want to help people?"

"Help yourself, Wren. One day you'll be grateful you did."

"I told you from the start that I wasn't going to be here for long. I was never planning to stay."

He nodded, the expression on his face impossible to read. He was shutting her out; she could tell from the way he looked at her, almost as if she was invisible. Like he was looking *through* her.

It hurt far more than she was prepared for.

"I'll send Quinn back in," he said. "She'll take you through what needs to happen next."

As he walked out of the meeting room and disappeared into the office, Wren blinked away tears. Perhaps it was for the best. She'd potentially damaged his career, lied to him and misled him… Why would he want anything to do with her after that?

You're doing the right thing. You're taking care of the people you care about.

But didn't she care about Rhys? Spending last night in his arms had made her feel so complete. So whole.

At that moment her phone started to vibrate and Kylie's face flashed up on the screen like a sign.

"Hey," she answered.

"Wren, I felt so bad about what I said last night." Kylie's voice was tight, her stress evident. "I'm sorry I told you not to call. I'm just… I'm messed up right now."

"It's fine. I shouldn't have pushed you," she said. "Anyway, I've almost wrapped things up here."

"Does that mean you're coming home soon?" The desperation in her friend's voice made a lump lodge in her throat.

"Your wish is my command."

"You don't know how happy that makes me. I miss you *so* much." She paused. "Are you okay? You sound upset."

"I'm fine. I'm just worried about one of the other interns," she said. It was the partial truth. Kylie didn't need the burden of Wren's relationship woes on her shoulders.

"Sean has been roughing her up and I think he's taken her paintings, too. He's got this whole scam on rotation."

"Shit. You figured that out, huh? I was too ashamed to admit that he convinced me to trust him. He was just so charming and nice, he said I had talent…"

"Kylie, you are *not* at fault for what happened to you. He took advantage of your trusting nature and he chose to abuse you. That is not on you." She paced the office. "I wish you'd talked to me about it…but I understand why you didn't."

"He made me feel like no one would believe me. Did you know his dad is a judge? He said even if I decided to report him nothing would happen because his father had gotten him off before."

"Son of a bitch," she muttered, shaking her head. She wasn't going to tell Kylie of her plans to help rope Sean into confessing; Kylie would only try to talk her out of it. "How's everything at home? Are you settling back in?"

"Yeah, I guess. I'm still really sore, but Debbie has been wonderful. She keeps visiting and bringing board games over to distract me. Last Saturday she skipped going out with her friends so we could have a movie night."

Wren said a silent thank-you to her sister. "She's got a big heart."

"So do you, Wren. Though I would have preferred you to be more like Debs and play games with me instead of going off on a vigilante mission."

"I don't want anyone else to go through what you went through."

"Me, neither." Kylie sighed. "But maybe I'm selfish and I just want my best friend to be here with me. It's much safer."

"We'll get him, Ky. I don't give a shit if his father is a judge, we're going to get proof of what he's doing." She swallowed. "He has your paintings, too, doesn't he?"

There was a sniffle on the other end of the line. "I should have said something to you about that, but he said he'd make me pay if I told anyone. I didn't even tell the therapist because I'm afraid he'll find me."

"He won't find you, Ky. I'm coming home to look after you."

"He said I owed him. That they were payment." Her voice sounded far away.

"We'll get them back, okay? I promise."

Rhys might be right about her always doing things for other people, but that was just who she was. Since it was clear he didn't understand that about her, it was probably best that she was heading back home.

A FEW DAYS later they were poised to make their final move on Sean Ainslie. Rhys had almost bitten his nails down to the quick. Technically, he wasn't supposed to be part of the team overseeing the surveillance of Wren's entry to Ainslie Ave. But he'd talked Owen into allowing him to observe in case anything went wrong from a technical standpoint.

Owen knew it was a bullshit excuse, but he hadn't argued. So long as Rhys didn't intervene in any way, he was free to observe.

They'd decided not to involve the police at this stage because it was unclear how deep of an influence Sean's father had. A corrupt judge would have many connections, and they didn't want to risk someone tipping him off. They just had to hope that Sean was cocky and stupid enough not to suspect Wren was taping him.

If he was going to bet on the reliability of anyone being stupid, it would be Sean Ainslie.

"She'll be okay, Rhys. I promise." Quinn placed a reassuring hand on his arm as they watched the screens capturing the footage from the gallery. "She's feisty. I appreciate that."

"I don't," he muttered, pretending to check his emails on his phone to avoid Quinn's raised brows.

"Bullshit, you love feisty women. How on earth would we be friends if you didn't?"

"You're my employee."

She rolled her eyes. "Next time you need help with a firewall, I'll remind you of this conversation."

"I told her not to do this." His stomach churned as the speakers wired to her mic crackled to life.

"Looks like she hasn't taken that advice."

He grunted. "It wasn't advice."

"What was it supposed to be? A command? I'm surprised she didn't tell you to shove it."

"I was looking out for her."

"No." She shook her head. "You're trying to instruct her how to live her life. Those are two different things."

"Are you saying I'm bossy?"

Quinn studiously tapped away at her laptop, making sure the recording function was set up for the Ainslie Ave cameras. "That would be putting it mildly."

"Gee, thanks."

"We're not friends, remember? I don't have to be nice to you."

God, he was really not in the mood for bantering with Quinn today. "I'm going to fire you one of these days."

She snorted. "I can see why she dumped your ass."

His head snapped up. "What the hell is that supposed to mean?"

How had she figured out that he and Wren were together? Nothing connected him to her except the conversation he'd had with Logan, and he was pretty sure his boss wasn't about to spread that information around.

"Logan said there were some complications in you working on this case. I get the impression you're not supposed to be here today."

He grunted in response.

"And I took the fact that you even knew her name to mean something was going on between you two." When he raised a brow she continued, "Normally you only care about the numbers. It's all stats and KPIs and closure rates. You never take an interest in the people side of things."

"You make me sound like a dictator."

"I get it, the numbers are an important part of your job. But there was mad tension in that meeting room when we were setting this whole thing up. Wasn't difficult to put two and two together."

He sighed and leaned back in his chair, turning away from Quinn's sharp, analytical gaze. "Doesn't matter now, anyway. As you said, she dumped my ass."

"Because you were a prick."

"That a fact or just an educated guess?" he said sarcastically.

"I'm gonna plead the Fifth on that one." She tucked her feet up under her so she was perched on the chair like some kind of punk Buddha. "So, you got in trouble, huh?"

"Dammit, Quinn. Are you trying to piss me off?"

"No." She held her hands up, but a smile tugged at the

corners of her lips. "Not at all. I'm kind of impressed actually. I've never seen you break the rules. Well, except for that one time where you accidentally put recycling into the regular trash can."

"Shut up."

"Seriously. You *never* push the boundaries. She's got to be one hell of a woman to tempt you to the dark side of employee misconduct."

Their argument was cut short when Owen called for a quick powwow over the speakers. He was near the gallery with Wren, making sure she was appropriately wired up. They had Jin, another senior security consultant, inside the gallery posing as a potential client in case things got nasty. Two more security consultants were positioned outside, ready to storm in if Jin or Wren needed backup.

But the layers of contingency didn't put Rhys at ease. He felt sick to his stomach that she was going to be walking in there to face that son of a bitch. But no amount of logical reasoning had been able to talk Quinn and Owen out of this plan. The thing was, if it had been anyone else in her place, he wouldn't have batted an eyelid.

Ainslie needed to be taken down and this *was* the best way to do it.

"Have you told her you care about her?" Quinn asked once Owen had stopped speaking.

"No," he admitted. Why would he when it was clear she never had any intention of staying? Nothing he'd done had changed that…so why cut himself open in front of her?

"No?" Quinn raised a brow. "Why not?"

"It's none of your business."

"You've been miserable ever since she offered to do this. I *know* what that feels like, trust me."

"Wren and I are not the same as you and your lover-boy."

"Maybe not. But you care about her and I haven't seen you care about many people. I have to wonder why that is."

"I made the right decision," he said, ignoring her comment. "It was tough but—"

"Yeah, yeah. Tough but fair. I'm familiar with the motto." She smiled and let the snarky expression drop. "Look, I'm not trying to tell you what to do. But, from one friend to another, maybe think about what that motto means. Tough doesn't necessarily mean you have to push people away."

"I know that."

But it was hard *not* to push people away, or at the very least keep them at a distance. It was easier not to get involved, not to risk anything. Still, Wren had managed to sneak past his barriers without him even noticing.

Pain wrenched in his chest. Why hadn't he tried harder to stop her? She didn't have the training for this. She was driven totally by her emotions and impulses, which meant she hadn't considered the consequences.

If something happened to her today…

She could get hurt and she'd have no idea how he felt; she'd have no idea that he loved her.

He sat stock-still as the truth burned through him. He loved her. It wasn't a shock; the feelings had been brewing for a while. But this was the first time he'd admitted to himself just how deep those feelings went.

What if he'd realized too late?

His gut twisted in response. Quinn was right; he'd tried to command Wren to live her life according to what *he* wanted. Instead of offering support like a decent person would do, he'd been a bossy asshole.

He made a promise then and there, as he watched Wren appear on the security-camera screen, that he would tell her he loved her when this was all over. No matter what, he would tell her.

16

WREN'S HANDS TREMBLED as she approached the gallery's front door. For all the bravado she'd mustered up when she'd decided to volunteer, not much of it had stuck around for the grand finale. She forced herself to think of Kylie and Aimee, how scared they must have been when they realized they were being played. That the man they'd fallen for was nothing more than a thief and an abuser.

She had to be brave for them.

Part of her had hoped that Rhys would be here to support her. The other part of her had been terrified that he'd show up and all her resolve would melt away. Last night she'd lain awake, tossing and turning with nerves, her stomach tied up in knots. The reality that soon she'd be leaving New York had washed over her, and instead of making her feel relieved, it made her want to cry.

She shoved the thoughts aside as she reached for the gallery door. Slowly, she drew in a steadying breath, and pushed.

The little bell above the door tinkled as she stepped inside, her head held high. This was it. All she had to do was get Sean to confess his crimes. It shouldn't be hard; he loved talking about himself. And now she had the leverage she needed to get him to confess the truth.

"Wren." Lola blinked from behind the reception desk. "What are you doing here? I thought you'd gone home to your family?"

A family emergency, that's what she'd told Lola to keep her in the dark. They couldn't risk any hint of the operation leaking to Sean. Not after the head of Cobalt & Dane had been forced to go to Sean Ainslie personally to make sure they were still employed by the gallery. Without the contract, they couldn't access the cameras.

"I need to speak with Sean," Wren said, hoping to hell her tone didn't reveal her nerves.

"He's just about to meet with a buyer." Lola nodded toward an attractive dark-haired man in a fitted black suit who was wandering around the gallery, looking at the paintings.

Wren recognized him as Jin, one of Owen and Quinn's colleagues. He was her safety net. The guy who was going to make sure she got out in one piece if Ainslie lost his shit.

"It's urgent," Wren replied.

"Gee, you guys don't make it easy for me," she said, shaking her head. "I can't believe you and Aimee both quit at the same damn time."

Aimee had quit? That news sounded too good to be true.

Lola picked up the phone and dialed the extension for Sean's office. Wren could hear his peevish tone even standing a foot away.

He won't get to treat anyone else like shit for much longer…

When he strode into the gallery, he ignored Wren and

walked straight over to Jin, hand outstretched. Then he motioned for Wren to follow him down the hall. Her heart leaped into her throat. Of course he wouldn't want to have the conversation out in the open—but how would Jin keep an eye on her if he took her out back?

"What the fuck do you want?" he asked. "If you've come here for your shitty canvas, I've thrown it out. Probably for the best. I'm not sure you have any talent."

"Then why did you hire me?" she asked, folding her arms across her chest carefully, so as not to obstruct the mic taped just inside of her blouse.

The tiny thing barely looked powerful enough to capture the voice of the person wearing it, but Owen had assured her that so long as she stood within a few feet of Sean it would record his voice, too.

"Because I liked looking at your ass," Sean replied with a cocky grin. "Too bad you haven't got anything of value from the waist up."

"Oh, so it wasn't to steal my paintings and pass them off as your own like you did with all the other girls who've worked here?"

Surprise streaked across his face but it was gone almost as quickly as it appeared. "You have no idea what you're talking about."

"Yes, actually, I do. I know everything, Sean. I know that you hire young girls from small towns because they're vulnerable and eager to please. I know that you steal their paintings and beat them up if they try to stop you. I know that you're a thief and a liar and you deserve to be put in jail."

His eyes darted around behind her. They were still in the hallway, but right at the back of the gallery. Jin wouldn't be able to hear what they were saying, but Owen would be communicating with him via an earpiece. She just had to trust that they were good at their jobs.

"And how are you so sure of all of this, Wren? Sounds like a great story to me. Maybe you should have been a writer instead of a painter."

"I've been in touch with your former employees. I spoke with Kylie and Marguerite. I've been speaking with Aimee."

At the mention of Aimee's name, a fire lit in his eyes and his mouth flattened into a thin line. "Bullshit."

"They told me that you keep the paintings in your storage room and you cover up their signatures and replace them with your own." Neither of them had said that directly, but it was an educated guess...one that was on the money if his thunderous expression was anything to go on. "Why do you do it? Is it because you have no talent of your own?"

His hand reached out so quickly she didn't have the chance to back away, and he caught her arm between his fingers. As he squeezed, pain shot through her.

"You're playing with fire, Wren. I know you're not smart, but let me spell it out for you." He leaned in so close that his breath heated her skin. Her stomach pitched violently but she managed to hold herself together. "You have nothing on me, you will *never* have anything on me and even if you did, I'm untouchable."

Wren felt a flutter of panic in her chest. Sean still hadn't given her anything incriminating. She needed to push him harder, get him to confess.

"No one is untouchable," she said. "It doesn't matter if your father is a judge. He can't save you from everything. How would he feel if he knew his son was an abusive bastard who preyed on young women? Don't you think he'd be disappointed in you?"

His fingers bore down on her, making her skin burn.

"You think he doesn't know?" Sean laughed. "I went to him after I messed Marguerite's face up just in case that mouthy bitch decided to go to the cops. Dear old Dad had a word with her and she didn't make a peep."

"So your father threatened some poor girl just to help you cover up what a piece of shit you are? I guess the apple doesn't fall far from the tree." She tried to pull her arm away but he held tight. So tight that the blood supply to her hand was being cut off. "What did you do with her paintings? Because it's not like you've made it big yet. Guess your plans aren't working out too well."

"I sold them," he said with a sneer. "Made fuck all, too. Guess she wasn't as talented as she thought."

"Or maybe you just haven't got a good eye. If you did, you would have been able to paint something decent yourself by now."

"Hardly," he snarled. "I'm scraping the bottom of the barrel with you worthless country girls. But I've found my golden ticket with Aimee."

Wren tried to shove him, her fear and anger bubbling over. But she was half his size. "You leave her alone."

"Maybe I'll work her over extra good tonight, just for you."

Tears pricked her eyes. "Please leave her alone."

"She's got what it takes, and I'm going to sell those paintings for all I can get."

"She'll leave you," Wren said, blinking through her blurry vision. "She'll realize she doesn't have to take this shit from you and she'll leave."

"No, she won't. I've got her locked up now and I'm

throwing away the key." The grin on his face was bordering on manic. "I made sure to do that after you got into her ear last time. So you can blame yourself for that one."

A sob wrenched out of her. "You're a monster."

"It's just business. Her paintings are going to make me rich."

At that moment footsteps sounded beside them and Sean released Wren so quickly her knees buckled and she dropped to the ground. Her arm throbbed as the blood started moving through it again.

"What the fu—"

"Keep your hands to yourself."

Wren looked up to see Jin pointing a gun straight at Ainslie. He stood over her, giving her a chance to stand up and scoot behind him.

"You okay, Wren?" Jin asked.

She nodded and Sean fumed at the both of them. "Get the fuck off my property. Now."

"You realize you've just admitted to holding someone against their will?" Jin said. "I thought you were despicable, but that takes the cake."

"We have to find her," Wren said, wrapping her arms around herself.

"We will. But first we're going to wait here until the NYPD arrives."

RHYS PACED THE length of his apartment, waiting for the Cobalt & Dane team to wrap up with Wren across the hall. Tonight they'd be putting her up in a hotel to make sure that she was safe—just in case Sean's father managed to get him out of holding.

Watching her go toe-to-toe with Sean had been one of the toughest things he'd ever done in his life. All he'd wanted to do was go to her, to step in front of her and protect her from that asshole. He'd wanted to dry the tears that had rolled down her cheeks once she'd finally gotten out of the gallery. Anything to make her feel better. Anything to make up for acting like a jerk when she'd volunteered to help take that bastard down.

All he could do now was hope that she'd hear him out when he told her how he felt.

After Ainslie had admitted to kidnapping Aimee, things had moved swiftly. Owen had called the police. Jin had an old buddy from his days with the NYPD who worked in the special victim's unit. They'd jumped on the case and had thankfully found Aimee within hours.

She'd seemed unharmed, but they'd admitted her to the hospital, anyway. She was in good hands now. As for Sean, he'd been taken into custody and would likely be charged with a slew of things, including kidnapping and assault.

Voices floated in from the hallway and Rhys recognized the calming tones of one of the counselors Cobalt & Dane regularly contracted. When the sounds faded to silence, he made his way to the front door. Owen had promised Rhys he could escort Wren to the hotel so long as he called the office as soon as Wren was checked in. He wasn't used to being micromanaged, but nothing could upset him now.

Sean was in custody. Wren was safe.

He walked over to Wren's apartment and knocked. This was it, confession time. When she swung the door open, he was greeted with a sight that almost tore his heart in two. Wren's face was swollen and puffy, and her cheeks were mottled with patches of pink and red.

"Don't stare at me like that," she said, dropping her

eyes to the floor. "I know I look hideous. I'm an ugly crier."

"You couldn't be ugly if you tried, Wren." He reached out and brushed his thumb along her cheek. "On the inside or the outside."

She held the door open for him, her eyes avoiding his. The second he stepped into her apartment he saw the small collection of boxes in the spot where her couch used to be. They were haphazardly stacked and didn't appear to be labeled.

"Heading home so soon?" he asked, fighting back the hurt that trickled through him like a toxin.

"Kylie is coming to get me tomorrow. Owen said they'd need me to come back at some point to testify against Sean, but I could go and be with my family for now." She drew her bottom lip between her teeth.

The careful speech he'd planned—and practiced—seemed to evaporate on the spot. He wanted to be with her more than anything, but facing her rejection was tearing him apart. Suddenly he felt like that desperate kid he'd always been, the one who'd craved his mother's attention. Who'd tried—and failed—to fit in with his new family. Who'd just wanted to be accepted.

"Are you taking me to the hotel?" She wrapped her arms around herself.

"Yeah." He nodded. "But, uh…I wanted to talk to you about something first."

"Sure. I haven't got anywhere for us to sit, though." She looked around. "And everything is all packed up so I can't make us coffee."

"I don't need any of that." He ran a hand over his hair and willed himself not to chicken out. "I wanted to apologize for the other day. I shouldn't have said the things I did."

"It's okay. I know I jump into some things headfirst." A smile tugged at her lips. "You can add 'impulsive' to my list of undesirable traits along with messy and clumsy."

"Wren, nothing about you is undesirable. The truth is, I was scared shitless about you going in there today. But more than that…" His mouth was suddenly drier than desert air. "I was lashing out because I was hurt. I was hoping you'd want to stay with me, and when you said you were going home I threw it back in your face."

"The things you said weren't exactly false. I *do* hide behind other people's problems." Her head bobbed. "I realized that today. I've spent so long 'not being good enough' that I felt like I needed to do things for people so they would like me."

"People like you for who you are, Wren. Not what you do for them."

"I understand that now. Kylie and Debbie will love me no matter what, and my parents still love me even though I might not be the successful child."

"What about *me*?" he asked, taking a step forward.

"What about you?" Her face tilted up, eyes wide.

The moment he reached for her hands he remembered all the things he wanted to say. "Do you know that I'll love you no matter what? Do you know that I'll do anything to be with you, Wren? I can't let you go without laying it out."

"You love me?"

"I do." He pulled her closer and she curled into him, her head resting against his chest. "You make me feel…

real. When you painted me, I was floored. No one has ever looked at me like that before."

"What do you mean?"

"Like they weren't trying to figure something out. When I was growing up, a lot of people would compare me to Marc or Mom. They didn't understand how I belonged, if I was adopted. If I was black or white. And then Mom didn't really look at me at all." He paused.

"I just painted what I saw."

"I like seeing myself through your eyes."

"Did you just compliment yourself?" She raised a brow and he laughed.

"I guess I did."

"Good. It's about time." Her fingers traced the buttons on his shirt. "You're so hard on yourself, it must be exhausting."

"It really is."

As he cradled her, the silk of her hair was soft under his palm. He was braced for her rejection, but painful as it would be, he knew he'd never forgive himself if he hadn't told her the truth.

"I can't figure out why someone like you would love someone like me," she said quietly. "I don't bring anything to the table. I barely function as an adult."

"You *are* an adult. Look at what you've done today—you do a lot of good, Wren. You're fearless. The world needs more people as strong as you."

"I don't care what the world needs, Rhys. I only care what you need."

"You." Rhys slid his hands up her neck and tangled them into her hair. "I need to wake up to your beautiful face every morning and see you looking at me like I matter. Like *we* matter."

"You're not going to change your mind?"

"No way. I've never needed anything more." His lips came down to hers, soft at first and then hungry. Desperate.

"I was going to come and see you before I went to the hotel."

"Really?" He brushed a strand of hair from her forehead. "What was your plan?"

"Silly, I don't do plans." She pressed her lips to his chest. "I had no idea what I was going to say. I just knew that I couldn't leave without asking whether you regretted the way we ended things. Because I did. I regret it so much."

"You don't have to regret it." He lowered his forehead to hers. "Stay."

"Okay," she breathed.

"Okay?" He never would have believed that such a benign word would one day cause the best change in his life.

"But first I need to go home and make sure Kylie and my family are okay after everything that's happened. Then I'll pack up my things and tell them that I'm moving here to be with the man I love."

"All right, but I'm coming with you."

"Deal." A laugh bubbled up in her throat. "What am I going to do for work when I'm back in New York? What about our living arrangements?"

"Listen to you with all those adult questions," he teased, bringing his mouth down to hers. "I must be rubbing off on you."

"Don't expect me to start a spreadsheet anytime soon." She screwed up her nose.

"So you love me, huh?"

Wren's eyes sparkled. "I do. You're the most kind-hearted, sexy, honest man I've ever met."

"Sexy, huh?" He wrapped his lips around her earlobe, heat surging through him when she moaned. "I like the sound of that."

"Well, we *do* have a hotel room at our disposal tonight." She grinned. "I'm assuming they have a bed frame, too."

"Oh, and here I was getting used to sleeping on the ground." He chuckled.

"Really?"

"No. It was awful."

She wrapped her arms around him and laughed. "See, didn't I say you were honest?"

Epilogue

Six months later

WREN TWISTED HER hands in front of her. Seeing her paintings up on a wall—knowing soon there would be people standing here, eyeing them critically—filled her with a strange mix of emotions. The art show was showcasing work from ten artists in total, all former employees—and victims—of Sean Ainslie.

When she'd headed back to Charity Springs with Rhys in tow, Wren had needed something positive to keep her busy. She had her man by her side, which had made her feel like the luckiest girl in the world, but she knew deep down that there was one more thing she could do to help Kylie and the other women who'd been hurt by Sean.

She straightened Rhys's portrait. It'd felt right to include it in the show; after all, it was the painting that had brought her back to art. That had made her want to be creative again. Without that painting she might have given up altogether.

But it wasn't really the painting that had healed her wounds. It was him. His hands, his mouth, his arms.

His love.

She'd wanted to do the same for the other women. So, she'd come up with the idea of the show to support Sean's victims, and hopefully to stop them from giving up their passion. To allow them to claim what was rightfully theirs.

Kylie and Debbie had taken on the tasks of organizing a space and getting the word out. Wren had rounded up the other artists. A few had declined, determined to keep that part of their lives in the past. Which she definitely understood. But eight had said yes, with three more agreeing to come along and support the cause. Wren had decided to ask for a small donation upon entry, with the proceeds to be given to a local charity for abused women.

"Everything looks amazing, Birdie," Debbie said, her hand slipping into Wren's. "This was such a wonderful idea."

"I hope it goes well. I don't want to let these girls down."

"You won't. Just the fact that you're doing this means so much to them, and it means the world to Kylie." Debbie rested her head on Wren's shoulder. "I know Mom and Dad don't always see why your art is important, but I do. You have a good soul and the way you share that is through your paintings. I'm so proud of you."

"Thank you." Wren pulled Debbie into a hug.

"Careful!" She touched a hand to her hair, laughing. "Do you know how much I paid for this blowout? Damn, Brooklyn is expensive. I have no idea how you're going to be able to afford to live here."

"I don't get blowouts at fancy salons, for one." She drew a breath, the nerves prickling along her limbs, filling her with buzzing energy. "And I got lucky—a local community center hired me based on all the volunteer work I'd done back home. They're not paying me a fortune, but it's something."

"I don't want to hear that you're living on baked beans and toast, okay?"

"So now you're my nutritionist as well as my doctor?" She nudged her sister in the ribs.

Having the support of her sister had made the move a lot easier. As for her parents…well, they loved her in spite of her impulsiveness, and that was all that mattered.

She glanced over to where Rhys stood talking to one of the other artists. He looked so handsome tonight in his dark suit and crisp white shirt. It made his brown skin gleam and his eyes sparkle. If they weren't at such an important event, she'd be dragging him out back so she could show him just how sexy he was. Just how much she loved him.

The word made a lump form in her throat. For an artist, the idea of love shouldn't be so scary, especially not when she'd survived having her work and reputation ripped apart by a whole town.

But it was utterly terrifying in the best way possible.

Earlier, she'd rounded up everyone involved in the show and they'd toasted with champagne to a successful evening. To triumph over horrible people and to never letting your dreams die. Seeing them all—especially Kylie—with smiles on their faces, nervously chatting and swapping stories about their art, warmed Wren.

Aimee hadn't been able to make it; she wasn't out of the woods physically or emotionally enough to face the past. But she'd sent her love in the form of a huge bunch of flowers and a promise that they would talk soon.

It was also great to see just how different everyone's

styles were. Kylie had her vegetables; Marguerite had the most beautiful garden landscapes. There were Fauvist birds, abstract flowers, Pop Art portraits. Then there were Wren's nudes, alongside Rhys's handsome face.

From a distance Wren could see the monochrome style of her paintings—all earth and flesh tones. It had taken her a long time to cultivate a theme for her work, to get comfortable in the voice with which she painted. But the people viewing her work seemed to be enjoying it.

"I can't believe you put my ugly mug up there with all those beautiful women." Rhys's voice ran down the length of her spine, making her shiver.

"I happen to think it's quite an attractive mug," she replied, turning to face him. "I wouldn't have painted it otherwise."

This close, she could easily breathe in the smell of soap and a bare hint of cologne on his skin. She'd come to crave that smell because it was uniquely him.

"This is an incredible thing that you've done, Wren. You've taken something ugly and transformed it into a thing of beauty."

"I know it won't change what happened to these women, I know that they'll always be affected by what he did to them. But if this helps them find the strength to keep going, then…that's a good thing, right?"

"Yeah, it's a good thing."

The sound of conversation and clinking glasses filled the air. The gallery was getting full, and all Wren wanted was to have Rhys all to herself. They had a hotel room close to the gallery for the night, a treat that he'd insisted on.

"I regret ever giving you a hard time for looking out

for other people," he said, his hand linking with hers. "You have such a kind soul. I really love that about you."

"Really? I thought you loved me for my brownies." She sipped her champagne and looked up at him, a smile tugging on the corner of her lips.

"Well, that too. Kindness and brownies, it's a good combination." He grinned. "In fact, it's such a good combination that I want to make sure it's part of my life forever."

"I'm not going anywhere..." Wren turned to give Rhys a playful shove when she noticed he'd dropped to one knee.

He held a box out to her, the plush velvet insert cradling a single, sparkling diamond that captured every color of the rainbow in its fractured light. "Wren Livingston, you're the best person I know. Your kindness and messiness is unsurpassable. I could not think of anything I want more than to spend the rest of my life living in your colorful, chaotic world."

"You do?"

All eyes in the gallery were now on her, the anticipation palpable in the air. Given Rhys's fear of rejection, his proposal was sweet on so many levels.

"One hundred percent."

"Not a hundred and ten?" She couldn't stop herself from laughing.

"There is no more than one hundred percent." He took the ring from the box and reached for her hand. The band was a perfect fit. "Will you marry me, Wren?"

"Yes," she breathed, and the whole room erupted in applause. As he stood, he swept her up into his arms and brought his lips down to hers.

"I guess I should have asked if you'd keep making me brownies for the rest of my life," he said as he pulled back.

"Too late. Bargaining time is over." She wrapped her arms around his neck. "You'll just have to take me as I am."

"That's all I've ever wanted."

* * * * *

Don't miss
MR. DANGEROUSLY SEXY,
the next book in
THE DANGEROUS BACHELORS CLUB *series,*
available February 2017!

REQUEST YOUR FREE BOOKS!
2 FREE NOVELS PLUS 2 FREE GIFTS!

Ⓗ HARLEQUIN®

Blaze

red-hot reads!

SPECIAL EXCERPT FROM

⬡ HARLEQUIN®

Blaze

*Erick Fields is shocked when prim and proper
Clover Greene agrees that sex should be part of their
"fake boyfriend" deal. She needed a buffer against he.
judgmental family, but this Thanksgiving she's getting
whole lot more!*

Read on for a sneak preview of
HER NAUGHTY HOLIDAY,
book three of Tiffany Reisz's sexy holiday trilogy
MEN AT WORK.

"I'm not going to try to convince you to do somethin
you don't want to do," Clover said.

"Why not?"

"Because no means no."

"I didn't say no. Come on. I'm a businessman. Let
haggle."

Clover laughed a nervous laugh, almost a giggle. Sh
sat behind her desk and Erick sat on the desk next to he

"You're pretty when you laugh," he said. "But you'.
also pretty when you don't laugh."

"You're sweet," she said. "I feel like I shouldn't hav
brought this up."

"So do you really need someone to play boyfriend fo
the week? It's that bad with your family?"

She sighed heavily and sat back.

"It's hard," she said. "They love me but that doesn
make the stuff they say easier to hear. They think they'.

aying 'We love you and we want you to be happy,' but
hat I hear is 'You're inadequate, you're a disappointment
nd you haven't done what you're supposed to do to make
s happy.'"

He grinned at her and shrugged. "You think I'm cute?"
e asked.

"You're hot," she said. "Like UPS-driver hot."

"That's hot."

"Smoking."

"This is fun," he said. "Why haven't we ever flirted
ith each other before?"

"You know, my parents would probably be very
npressed if they thought I were dating a single father.
hey'd think that was a ready-made family."

"You really want me to be your boyfriend?" Erick
sked. He already planned on doing it. He'd do anything
or this woman, including but not limited to pretending to
e her boyfriend for a couple days.

"I would appreciate it," she said.

"We can have sex all week, too, right?"

"Okay."

"What?" Erick burst into laughter.

"What?" she repeated. "Why are you laughing?"

"I didn't think you'd say yes. I was joking."

"You were?" Her blue eyes went wide.

"Well…yeah. I mean, not that I don't want to. I do
ant to. I swear to God, I thought you'd say no. I never
uessed you'd say yes, not in a million years."

"And why not?"

Don't miss HER NAUGHTY HOLIDAY
*by Tiffany Reisz, available November 2016 wherever
Harlequin® Blaze® books and ebooks are sold.*

www.Harlequin.com

Reading Has Its Rewards

Earn **FREE BOOKS!**

Register at **Harlequin My Rewards** and submit your Harlequin purchases from wherever you shop to earn points for free books and other exclusive rewards.

Plus submit your purchases from now till May 30th for a chance to win a $500 Visa Card*.

Visit **HarlequinMyRewards.com** today

Earn **FREE** REWARDS Join Today! HarlequinMyRewards.com

MYR16

HARLEQUIN®

A *Romance* FOR EVERY MOOD™

Love the Harlequin book you just read?

Your opinion matters.

Review this book on your favorite
book site, review site, blog or your own
social media properties and share
your opinion with other readers!

Be sure to connect with us at:
Harlequin.com/Newsletters
Facebook.com/HarlequinBooks
Twitter.com/HarlequinBooks

HARLEQUIN®

A *Romance* FOR EVERY MOOD™

JUST CAN'T GET ENOUGH?

Join our social communities
and talk to us online.

You will have access to the latest
news on upcoming titles and special
promotions, but most importantly,
you can talk to other fans about your
favorite Harlequin reads.

Harlequin.com/Community

Facebook.com/HarlequinBooks

Twitter.com/HarlequinBooks

Pinterest.com/HarlequinBooks